ORPHANED

ORPH

ELIOT

ANED

SCHREFER

SCHOLASTIC INC.

Copyright © 2018 by Eliot Schrefer

This book was originally published in hardcover by Scholastic Press in 2018.

ISBN 978-1-338-60831-1

10 9 8 7 6 5 4 3 2 1   20 21 22 23 24

Printed in the U.S.A.   40
This edition first printing 2020

Book design and illustrations by Abby Dening

FOR DR. JANE GOODALL

"THE MORE YOU LEARN ABOUT THE DIGNITY OF THE GORILLA, THE MORE YOU WANT TO AVOID PEOPLE."

—DIAN FOSSEY

GORILLA VOCALIZATIONS

hoo: *acknowledging the peace of a repetitive life*
wragh: *expressing intimidation*
acha: *loving and knowing something well*
mrgh: *wanting to kill*
amrcha: *wanting to kill something loved and known well*

CENTRAL EASTERN AFRICA

600,000 YEARS AGO

Until this time, gorillas lived by the millions in a broad band of jungle across Africa. Then a series of volcanic eruptions, many times more forceful than any the modern world has experienced, occurred in the Great Rift Valley. The shift in landscape allowed tribes of early humans to travel south into this area for the first time.

It would be the first meeting between ape and human.

PART ONE

HOME

Rock. Nut.
Snub looks between the two, thinking.
This tree keeps its nuts high in its branches—
a fallen one is a lucky treat.

She imagines rolling the inside nugget in her mouth,
biting its oily flesh.

Tongue between her teeth, brow scrunched,
she raps the rock on top of the nut.
It does not crack.

She licks the rock.
The rock tastes like rock.
She licks the nut.
The nut tastes like dirt.

Snub twists the woody halves.
They will not part.

Opening nuts is Mother's job,
but Mother let Snub go off alone.

mrgh.

Fresh fury surges.
Snub hurls the nut, aiming
at a pair of magpies.

It goes wide and disappears into the foliage.
Worthless nut.

Snub looks to see if anyone has
been impressed by her rage.
But this only reminds her:

Her family is not here.

The magpies don't fly away.
The magpies watch and mock.
The magpies are not afraid of Snub.

Snub grunts and charges.

The birds flutter up,
chopping white and black
into the open blue sky.

As she watches them flee,
Snub feels better.
When she leaves the clearing,
she struts.

Maybe when she returns to her family,
they will be impressed by her.

When Snub finds her family,
not a single one of them looks up.

Brother is feasting on the buds of a thicket.
Wrinkled and Teased, the squabbling older females,
are back-to-back in a patch of clover,
searching out the lightest greens.

Mother hasn't stirred.
Her night nest has become a day nest.
This is not like Mother.

Mother
is no longer
like Mother.

Snub knows what is to blame.
It is that thing.
It is pink
and it wriggles.
It is pink
like a large worm.
Mother should crush it
under her foot.
Ooze under her toes!

But instead
Mother is caring for it.

It used to be
that Snub only had
to worry about
foraging food and
being close to Mother.

It used to be
that Snub and Mother
groomed each other,
climbed trees with linked arms,
passed a fruit rind
until together they had stripped it
of every glossy golden morsel.

It used to be
that when all this was done
they would sprawl in the sun-fragrant grass,
content.

hoo.

Then the worm arrived.

Now Mother doesn't allow Snub to come near.
Now Snub hasn't been touched all day.
Now Snub's legs crumple right where she stands.
Now Snub lands heavily at the edge of the family's clearing.
Now Snub is outside everything that used to be
inside

and she doesn't understand why.

Snub knows what will happen next,
knows she will be unhappy after,
but she cannot stop herself.

She gets to all fours,
feet furrowing rich black soil,
and cheats her way to Mother.
She leans so the hairs on her back mingle with Mother's,
extends an arm,
as
slowly
as
she
can,
until it grazes Mother's knee.

Mother tightens her grip on the pink worm.
As she pivots, Mother's eyes look at Snub
but don't see Snub.

Snub still doesn't understand why.
She has done nothing wrong,
not once this day has she
kicked Brother
teased Wrinkled
pelted Mother
yanked Silverback.

Snub stares out at everything that is not Mother:
one puff of cloud in the sky,
moss on the trees, thick as wet green hair,
bright edges of a puddle,
fly-milled soil, so richly black that it foams.

Snub can't bring herself to say

hoo,

because Mother is ignoring her
and might not

hoo

back.

Snub stands.
Snub sits.

Snub tries
one more time
to lean against Mother.

Snub's breath catches.
Mother has let her stay beside her!

Snub risks lowering her shoulders
so she is curled around Mother's body.

Mother allows that, too!

The worm isn't just pink.
Fine black hairs drape along it.
Its eyelids don't quite close over the slick slivers of its eyes.

It is a weak and fragile and useless and disgusting thing,
even if Snub sees now that it's a small version of a gorilla.

Surprise:
She wants
to hold this tiny gorilla that came out of her mother,
to cradle its tiny shoulders in her rough palm,
to pry its eyes open and see them look into hers,
to say

acha,

to share in Mother's

acha.

Mother sneezes.

Afraid that she is about to be alone again,
Snub holds very still.
Startled by Mother,
the worm raises its too-heavy head,
then feeds some more.
Feeding makes Snub think of food.
She selects a handful of sweet grass
and sprinkles it on the baby's face.

The baby is too useless to eat this grass.
The pink-gorilla-baby-worm doesn't *do* anything
except take away Mother.
If Mother doesn't start foraging soon
she won't eat anything before the day goes dark
and her day nest will turn into a night nest.
This fragile little thing,
which demands

acha

and gives none back,
will keep Mother in this one spot for the whole day.
It makes Snub growl out loud—

mrgh

but softly, so Mother cannot hear.

Snub rolls away from Mother
and knucklewalks through the clearing,
blowing contempt through her nostrils.

The day ages.

Already heavy with humming insects,
the jungle thickens until it is murky with their sound.
The sun lowers beneath the tops of the trees,
its light disappearing as quick as a thought.
Snub hasn't eaten enough today,
and she knows she'll wake before light with a hollow ache,
her belly plump and sharp.

Alone again,
no longer a daughter but nothing else either.

Is there more out there than this family?

In the morning, Snub puts her mind on Brother.

Brother lags behind the world.

He eats buds, grunting with wonder
each time he peels back a sap-stiff frond
to discover—surprise!—yet another soft brown center.

Snub rocks from side to side,
feet in Brother's face,
hoping he will notice.

Brother does not notice.

Snub rocks harder, until she tumbles right into him.
He grunts and splays out, flat in the grass,
looking at Snub in shock.
Then he rasps and gets up on all fours,
waiting for her to start the game up again.
Why does he never rock into *her*?

Snub bowls right into him, and this time knocks him flat.
He gets up, rasp-laughing and expectant.
Playing with Brother will always be a one-sided game.
No gorilla in the family plays the way Snub wants to play.

While the other gorillas—
Silverback, Brother, Wrinkled, and Teased—
begin their nests, Snub makes slow circles around Mother.

It used to be that they nested together.
Now Mother wants only to be with Silverback and the worm,
and it hurts like a hole where there once was a tooth.

Now that she has the pink worm,
Mother settles in close to Silverback,
bedding in a sheltered stretch between his hulking body
and the sun-warmed side of a tree.

Silverback lies serenely on his haunches,
expressing no

                                                 acha

or

                                                 mrgh

or

                                                 wragh.

He flicks his eyes to the pink worm baby,
tenderness wisping on his face.
Snub paces near, hoping Silverback and Mother will look up,
will waggle their chins in that way that means

Yes, come and be with us.

But Silverback makes no such move.
Mother makes no such move.
She still looks at Snub like Snub is no longer Snub.

Steam and boom.

Sky red and black, and a pink worm,
suckermouth gaping,
not for Mother but for Snub.

The dream ruptures and spits Snub out.
She sits up, grunting, patting the moss around her,
beating her chest against sweaty stirrings.

For the first time, the night is not dark.

It is not the gray white of moonlight on low clouds either.
It is red.
A jumping red.
A painful red.
A red like the inside of a tree that lightning has struck.
A red to hurt.

The horizon blooms into the sky
and Snub watches the red bend and expand,
plume up to take on sparks of yellow,
orange clouds massing high above the earth.

The other gorillas scatter from the noise,
but Snub wants to see those beautiful reds up close.

She surges up the hill and sees a monkey
stirred out of sleep,
staring up at the sky, hands over its ears.
The monkey's fear gives Snub fear.

She cries out,
and the ground responds.

The mountain has always been as permanent
as the sky,
but now it moves.
Rocks crack and heave,
like the land is laboring through some sickness,
buckling at the seams of its wound.

The mountain makes sizzling, suffering sounds.
It begins to bleed down its slope.
Even though it is still far away,
Snub can feel that the blood is hot.

The air booms, afraid like Snub.
She pivots, hooting. Where is Silverback? Where is Mother?

Snub punches a puddle,
sends up a spray of muddy water and blue-black flies.
She hoots and calls,
but she cannot hear or see or smell Silverback.
Her curiosity about the mountain's distant suffering
has brought her too far.
She is lost.

A small gorilla by herself at night might die,
and finding her family will take time.
Snub knows it will be best to hide away up here,
as still as possible,
and make her way down in the morning.

She rips up tufts of moss and piles them lumpily,
then harrumphs down into the mess.

Day brings
terror of wandering.

The sick distant mountain has
gone back to the color
a mountain should be,
but Snub's worried heart
has not gone back to the speed
a heart should be.

hoo

is as far away
as her family.

The air is drier and cooler up here.
Snub's lungs feel rough,
like their insides have skidded along the ground.

Once, when she looks back down the slope,
her mind sees Mother coming to find her.

But it is only the shadow of a frond.

A hawk circles.
The sun slants.
The day will soon end.

The ground goes sandy and firm.
Cool edges of rock cut Snub's feet
wherever her hair parts between her toes.

She reaches the top of a ridge and hoots in wonder
at the sight of a new place.

The green continues farther than Snub
thought green ever could,
vibrant all the way to a ridge of mountains,
capped by snow and forbidding cliffs.

No gorilla could ever pass that way.

For comfort,
Snub looks back
to the familiar green basin where her family lives,
the brown lake in the center where Silverback
sometimes leads them to cool and splash.

For curiosity,
Snub turns forward
to the new land edged in mountains.
From far below she can hear
the muffled call of a forest elephant.

Brother would run right now,
fear dung clodding his legs—
Wrinkled or Teased or Silverback would run—
When she was with them, Snub would have run, too—

But by herself, she finds out what Snub alone will do,
faced by a new place.

Snub alone is *curious*.

She hoots, lost between thrill and terror.
She turns a slow circle, not sure what to do with herself.
One moment she's looking down into the green crater where
her family is somewhere bedding down without her,
the next moment she's peering into this new land
where elephants call.

Snub builds a nest before the sun vanishes,
staring out into unfamiliar jungle.
Maybe she will never find her family.

Maybe this is all that Snub will ever have:
trees draped in spiderwebs,
a trio of yellow parrots,
a small brown antelope nibbling on lichen,
a burnt heaviness to the air the only sign
of the suffering mountain that set Snub
running
away from her family.

Snub does not feel any

acha

for those animals,
but maybe she could.

Maybe

acha

doesn't have to be
only for other gorillas.

Here, she is alone.
With her family, she was abandoned.

Maybe alone is better than abandoned.

Snub's eyes are already open when,
like a fruit's dark rind,
the night cracks to reveal a ring of yellow dawn.
Mists have sloughed from the mountains
that rim the gorillas' green land.
As Snub rolls in her nest, trees
disappear and reappear,
released and retaken,
the mists unsure of what they want to keep.

Snub thought the distant mountain's suffering was over,
but that night it suffers again.

Another boom rolls Snub down a slope
as if the black smoke has grown
arms and fingers
and shoved.
In the tumbling dark of
sharp rocks,
broken roots,
breast-beats of wind,
she grasps
nettles,
vines,
clods,
creatures that sting and squirm away
but slow her all the same.
Snub stands shakily,
swallows sour terror,
beats her chest once and then twice,
returning fear to the mountain.
It is only when she stops that she thinks,

What if the delirious mountain
staggers forward?

What if the mountain
carries its misery
to her family?

Broad, flat stone beneath feet and hands.
Nighttime ledge overlooking the lake.

Snub's family has been on the daytime ledge,
has overlooked the daytime lake.
She smells them here.

Snub rises to two feet and beats her chest.
She heaves in deep gasping breaths,
undone by the undoing of the world,
her body nettling
where her reckless journey has split her skin.
She whimpers as she breathes,
her ribs a bruised and jagged place.

Her own sounds return over
murmurs of lapping moonlit water.

She beats her chest again.

Thump thump.

  (Pap pap.)

Silverback!

Thump thump.

  (Pap pap.)

Snub races along the lake's edge,
tracing his sound.

The suffering mountain is getting closer,
sprays of earthblood filling the sky,
streaking lines of red over the lake's surface,
too close now to be beautiful.

A hulking space of no light.
It cries to intimidate:

wragh!

Here is the pungent odor of Silverback's fear.
Snub buries her face in his hair,
wraps hands and feet around wrists,
takes him as shelter.

Silverback's hands are on her,
picking through her injuries.

It makes her pain greater, but her worry is less.

The mountain is merciful.
Maybe it saw Snub's worry
and stopped suffering
before it could lumber into her family.

It sends out smoke, a few wisps,
like whimpers to remind everyone
what it has gone through.

Maybe Snub's leaving won't undo the world after all.

Frogs croak as murky lake water laps against reeds.
A bee lands on a length of bamboo husk.
An eagle cries against the blank and settled sky.
How was Snub ever dissatisfied by this?

When Silverback rolls out of the clearing,
Snub follows,
trailing her fingers along the tips of grasses,
enjoying their softness.

Every sensation that was once not enough
is now a source of

hoo.

Teased and Wrinkled barely look up.
They scarf green leaves,
doing the strange thing that only these
old gorillas do,
humming joy to their food.

Mother is here,
but Snub doesn't have the courage
to look at her yet,
to find in Mother's eyes
    anger
    sadness
or worse:
    no feeling at all.

Mother.

She is resting against a tree,
the baby asleep on her belly.

acha!

Snub chews air.
She pulls up thistle but forgets to bring the stalks to her mouth,
strewing a purple trail of broken flowers.
She drops the limp stems left in her sweaty palm on Mother's
    belly,
all over the baby.

An offering.

Mother grunts and turns away.

The baby picks up a palm-softened stalk and gums it,
peering at his own hands in surprise.

When Snub reaches a finger to him,
five perfect little fingers grasp it,
pollen dusting each black knuckle.

acha.

Ground shakes.

Fear sets Snub still and alert,
focuses her attention on Silverback.
Mother retreats to Snub,
presents her back for comforting.

Snub feels Mother's infant
under her hands for the first time,
though she's too nervous for any feeling of

acha.

Silverback feints one way and then another,
facing off against the invisible enemy
somewhere under the earth.

Only Snub has seen up close
the red torture that ripped out of the mountain.

Only Snub knows
that if that enemy has now come
to rip her family open
with its spurts of hot red,
not even Silverback will be able
to defeat it.

The air
   is bitter.
The air
   smells like the underside of a sunned rock.
The air
   sets hairs prickling and tall.
The air
   brings Silverback lunging at shadows.
The air
   makes fingers squirm through black hair.
The air
   makes Brother hide his face in Snub's belly.

A startling rush, a flapping tremor.

The two magpies Snub once hurled a rock at
are flying over the family,
cawing raucously.

Those clever magpies are fleeing.

A new sound from the earth,
like it is belching air,
like it has eaten shiny green leaves
without licking soil first
to prepare its stomach.

Even Silverback is scared
by this new strange sound.
Dung puddles beneath him.
Smoke rises against blue.
The sun become a pale flower bulb.
Dusk arrives at midday.

From the lake above,
a troop of monkeys shrieks,
arrives darting in the trees.

One tumbles past,
yelping in pain,
steam rising from its fur.

Snub is the only one who turns
toward danger.
Her family searches for the ghosts of

hoo,

between mossy rocks and among the bamboo stands
where they foraged and napped.

When the sky itself is the source of fear,
and sky is everywhere,
where can gorillas go?

Only when the mountain rests
can the family eat.

Bright bitterness of dark leaves,
watery sweetness of younger buds.

Busy eating, Mother doesn't notice
that the baby has one hand on Snub.
He lifts his other set of tiny fingers,
laces them into Snub's wiry hair.

Feet in Snub's hair now, too,
so that the baby is dozing,
gripping only her.

Snub stares at him,
ignoring the pain in her cricking neck,
the stabs from her scabbing wounds.
She breathes onto his face,
watches his long eyelashes flutter.

Snub pulls the baby to her ribs,
like she has seen Mother do.
She strokes his smooth hair,
watches his little eyebrows unfurrow.

Mother works her eyeteeth
under bamboo bark
to get at the sweet food beneath.

Snub takes a chewed-up ball of green
from her own mouth
and pins it between her lips
so she can waft it under the baby's nose.
He gums it.
Snub gives a sound ripe with satisfaction.

acha.

A moment stretches long in Snub's mind:

hoo.

Eating clover with Silverback and Mother,
Brother pulling Teased's hair.

Then the earth itself is the branch of a tree,
breaking under an untried weight.

It rolls the family
down a new slope of ruined ground,
tumbles them and crashes them.

Mother's toes dig into the flesh of Snub's thigh,
then they're ripped away.

The water follows.

The lake is attacking,
sending its brown waters
rushing down.

Those waters suck through the jungle trees,
ripping up saplings,
whipping them into the mud.

Even as Snub spins and tumbles,
she sees the delicate white neck of an egret
struggling to free itself
but caught in a lashing wet vine

and dragged under,
its pale curve disappearing under tree-high
churns of brown and black and green.

Snub's world is sky
and then mud
and then sky.

Dark chaos.
Silverback roars,

mrgh!

Gurgling and splashing.
A roar choked off.

A tree sloughs through the water, and though Snub

leaps

its roots snag her
and pull her
under the surface.
She drags herself onto the tree,
scrambles again when its trunk rolls her under,
climbs into the nest of its roots.
Snub's ears are ringing,
and her mind can't straighten the world.
Everything is on a tilt,
and the tilt itself is tilting.
She travels the river this way,
a gorilla
floating on the water
like a bug,
the land

too far to reach.

Snub struggles to understand
how a lake can fall.

Where there once had been a hillside
now there is a waterfall.
Trees bow and stagger in its flood.

Snub sees white bellies of dead fish,
and the green-brown of fish
that have not yet died,
that still show their correct side to the world.

More and more flood, a river
seizing the shore, taking it
farther from Snub even as
she staggers toward it.

The upturned ground is too far to reach.
Unaccustomed creatures writhe on it:
giant earthworms and millipedes,
ants everywhere, as constant as dirt,
scrambling over the glowing dots of their eggs,
a nest of pink rodents
writhing through the earth,
so young their blue eyes
are still skinned over,
feeling for their mothers.

Where is Mother?

The water slows.

The insects are all silent.
Snub has never heard
the world without insects.

The water is not water
on the surface.
It is ash, thick and gray,
swirling and chunking.

Snub sends a cry of

wragh

into the upturned world:
Where is her family?

The uprooted tree turns a corner,
and she is no longer alone.

A small body is there,
lodged among the branches
of a tree bowing against the flood.

Wet through, the baby
looks even more like a pink worm than before.
His body is limp,
fingers and toes pointing to the water,
as if some much larger creature
has discarded him.

Snub hoots.
There is no answer.
She feels a keening sense of worry, says

acha

for the wretched thing

hoping the baby will hear her
if it can hear anything
anymore.

Snub's tree is floating
down the wrong side of the river.
It will not go close enough.
To save the baby,
she must leave the safety
of the floating tree.

She will do it.

When she eases off,
her bottom half disappears
into the wet ashy gloom.
She's left the tree that kept her from
swallowing water
at the bottom of the flood.
The river is mostly cold,
though ribbed with currents of hot.
Around her legs
Snub can feel
rocks,
thistle and trees,
slithers of creatures,
slithers of vines.
The ash is soft,
like the inside of a mouth.
She tries to leap toward the baby in the tree
but her feet push against

ground that is more slippery than she thought,
plunge
into cold brown water.
Instinct brings her to all fours,
even deeper under the river.
Her throat fills with mud
before she can stop herself
from taking a breath.
Her body is too heavy
to get to the surface,
no matter how much she kicks and punches.
She hurls herself
     —for one lung-gashing instant
     she's above water,
     tries to gulp in air
     but only gargles mud—
She's down again.
Her shoulder lands in a sludgy thicket
of drowned ferns,
and her fingers grip their roots.
Pull.

Snub has been saved
by slick and muddy green.

Snub hugs the trunk
to ease her aching shoulders,
then places one hand and the other
higher up the tree,
reaching for the little creature.

Climbing a tree is familiar,
even in this changed world.
Climbing a tree
makes her say

hoo.

The baby
is flat across the branch,
arms and legs dangling,
like he's asleep.

But he is not asleep.

Snub places a finger underneath
his tremoring chin,
examines it and lets it rest.

She wraps a long-fingered hand
around his rib cage,
carries him as gently
as an overripe fruit.
Against her breast,
like Mother would do.

Snub calls out loudly,
hoping her family will come.
Even Brother would be helpful.
But there is no response.

She will leave the river with this little gorilla fruit,
as water-plump as a fallen pear.
Gorillas are meant to be on land.
Even gorillas who don't move anymore.

Snub curls the little body around her neck,
slots her fingers between bumps of spine.
The muscles in her legs,
already exhausted,
burn in the cold river water.

She lands heavily on her back
in a stand of fronds,
sending out a brown cloud of crickets.

Broken reeds stab her back,
but the baby is safe against her belly.
His eyes quiver beneath delicate black lids.
His throat bobs, and a tendril of muddy brown
emerges from the corner of his lips,
running over Snub's elbow.

She holds his feet high, so the ooze might drain out.
The baby's eyes flutter open
and he coughs,
baby-warm ash splattering Snub's elbow.

She presses him close to her breast.
He gums her nipple,
then his head dangles back.

He is alive.
He is asleep.

Snub stares and stares at his face.
Snub has saved Mother's baby.

He is still the ugliest creature she's ever seen.

Snub shifts her arm
so it covers the sleeping baby more.

Her eyes close, as heavy as his.
She wakes without realizing she fell asleep.

Snub is in a well of soft sunshine,
snorting as something tugs her nostril.
It is a little gorilla finger,
exploring the flat lobes of her nose.

She will never hate him again.
He is no longer a pink worm.
He becomes Breath.

She pulls Breath closer to her.
He settles into her grasp,
trying again for her nipple
but not finding milk.

Birds fly from the suffering mountain,
sharp flares of black against heavy banks of gray.
White flashes from the tips of wings.
Maybe those two magpies are in there.

As she watches them pass,
Snub's eye spots a patch of wild celery,

smashed in the tumult,
fragrant stalks splaying in every direction.

Soon her belly is full.

A pond where once was none,
water a brown so deep
it is nearly the black of rot.

The tips of drowned ferns sway
on the water's ashy surface.

Sooty cormorants fidget,
spreading their wings and strutting,
yellow throat pouches trembling
as they balk at strange water.

Buffalo mill at the far edge,
lowing and sipping,
the water's surface darkening
the sweeping curve of their horns.

They are focused on the jungle
where there is a sound of
yip.
It sets Snub's hairs standing.

A hot wind whips down the slope,
wakes the flesh on Snub's cheeks,
tingles her hands and chest.

She faces away from it,
curving her body over Breath's.

On the spot of ground between her big toes, she sees
a young tendril of vine wither and curl into itself
as heat from the mountain
makes Snub's heart surge.

Without another thought
she is racing down the slope
toward the dark pond,
away from the red.

Making sure Breath is secure on her back,
Snub stands up on two legs and beats her chest,
hitting the spot where her heart is already
pounding.

Pap pap

Pap pap

like Silverback would do.

He is not here, and some gorilla
must always be Silverback.

The mountain rumbles and sends
wind,
fast and searing,
crisping and dry.

Snub runs from it,
fear making her shambling and fitful.
She falls more than she races.
Breath whimpers his panic.

The hot wind turns trees limp
and then, sizzling, bends them.
Even though she is facing away,
the pain closes Snub's eyes.

Her heart knows this hot wind
is like a buffalo chasing her down,
horns lowered.
The angrier its snorts are,
the more she must not look back.
Looking back is to slow,
and to slow is to die.

The gray sky
starts falling to the ground,
rolling misty boulders
in all directions,
fast and sure.

The ash keeps easy pace with her,
and then it is beyond her,
clogging Snub's vision
with its sooty gray.

Snub vaults bodies without knowing what animal has fallen,
only that the fallen creature is warm and maybe even still alive
but has succumbed to the water or the tumbling or the ash.
She will not let the same thing happen to her or Breath.

A smell both sweet and revolting
distracts Snub enough that a palm bush
emerges unexpectedly from the swirling gray
and smashes her.

Breath squeals in fear.
When Snub gets up
she sees that the hairs
along her arm
are smoking.
It is her own body
causing the burning smell.

A forest antelope plunges
down the mountainside,
fleeing the red.

When it strikes a tendril of fire,
it does not drown.
It does not struggle to get back onto the land.

One delicate hoof hits the red flow,
then the animal is a blaze of yellow flame,
flaring and disappearing.
It has not become dead.
It has become gone.

Snub hides in the pond water,
billowing ash raining thickly,
turning Breath the color of pith.
The shore of the pond,
once only a few lengths away,
has vanished.
Sounds are all that
tell her of others,
lowing buffalo,
yipping dogs,
shrieking parakeets,
barking baboons.
She edges Breath away from the worst of the noise,
creatures slithering against her waist and legs.
The tail of a buffalo emerges in front of her, and

the beast kicks out and startles away,
barely missing Snub.
She has been on two feet for too long—
her hips ache.
She moves Breath so he is riding on her shoulders.
He wraps his hands around her forehead,
little finger drifting into her view.
Insect carcasses strew the ashy pond.
They, too, steam as they float,
clumping around bobbing logs.
Some of the insects are still alive.
Snub ignores them even as she feels them
thrash in the hair on her cheeks
and over her brows.

Breath catches a stick bug in his hand,
brings it to his mouth.
Snub can see flailing insect legs,
until she hears a crunching sound
and the legs go still.

Snub wades blind,
eyes scrunched closed,
until she hears heavy breathing.

She's staring into the eyes of a hippopotamus.
The bulging and blundering animal,
so puffed and ungainly on land,
is a gorilla-killer in the water,
more dangerous than any crocodile.

But this animal has flared wide nostrils
at the end of its bulbous head,
snorting into the water hard enough
to send up sprays of muck.

Its soft brown irises are framed in white
as it stares at the suffering mountain.
The hippopotamus is terrified.

They stare at one another,
Snub and Breath and hippopotamus,
undone by their changed world.

The beast surges away.

The dome of ash tightens and darkens.
Even the fastest creature could not outrun it.

wragh.

Snub cries to the hot sky.
She can't hear any answer.
If her family is nearby,
they are not telling her.

She can breathe only shallowly.
Anything deeper and the heat gashes,
pulling her into a fit of coughing.

She whimpers, hoping Mother
or Brother or Wrinkled or Teased
or Silverback
will hear her distress and come.

But if they are here,
she cannot see them.

All she can do
is wait
and hope
her family will appear with the dawn.

PART TWO

FAR FROM HOME

This night brings more to see instead of less.

Other hues appear behind the ash.
The sky is rimmed red in one direction,
a gurgling growth of angry color,
like a pustule.

The suffering mountain
that used to be home
is now so far away.

It brings a warped, tense feeling,
the opposite of

hoo.

Carefully holding a sleeping Breath,
Snub eases herself deeper into the slackening water,
now the same dark as the clogged sky,
though lapped in moonlight.

Husky breathing stills her.
She almost grunts,
but stops herself.

It is not a gorilla that she's heard.

Rain comes.
Snub normally hates getting wet
but is glad for the rain now,
for the familiar patter of droplets hitting water,

for the rivulets running down her forehead
that smell like ash but leave her clean.

Somehow, time passes during this watchful night.

The sun can only glimmer
behind the clouds of ash.

But with its rise she can hear sounds of gorillas,
gorillas that may be her family.

When will full daylight come?

Logs
sticks
leaves
insects
white bellies of fish
white bellies of lizards
white bellies of mice
rats
birds
monkeys
dead and alive,
all glint in thick ash sludge.

This dark pond is the reason Snub is still alive,
but the dark pond is full of death.

She must cross it to bring Breath
to the sound of Mother.

This little body
in her aching arms
is the courage she needs.

Snub rubs the top of Breath's head until he is awake.

He is dazed and groggy, but his eyes are open.

Breath spooks at the dark, filthy water.

He is angry, pinching and biting her.

Snub moves him up to her shoulders.

He goes mute.

Breath's small fingers grip tight.

He shivers as his back hits a raft of dead birds.

Snub moves toward the sound of

                                                            hoo.

Snub passes a crocodile
and a troop of long-toothed baboons.

Snakes plane through the water,
slithering as easily through pond as land,
triangle heads leaving
delicate wakes
through ash sludge.

A seething mass of red ants.
They've made their own raft,
those on the bottom struggling
to get to the surface,
those on the surface
sending the bottom to drown.

Fire ants can swarm and kill.

But none of these animals attack one another.

The mountain's suffering has remade the world.

She is almost there.

As she nears the gorillas, Snub's heart lifts,
but to keep her and Breath safe
she fights not to make
any sounds of

acha.

There is Silverback!
A patch of his hair has burned away,
but he is whole.

There is Teased!
She looks exhausted, older than ever,
head drooping while she hunkers down.

Other gorillas are on the far side of Silverback,
but Snub cannot tell which ones.

Snub has made a sound of

acha!

before she knows it.

Birds and insects go quiet.

Snub looks back at the crocodile
and sees only the flash of its tail as it dives.

Maybe it is coursing right toward her.

Snub grips Breath tight,
picks up speed,
racing through wet clutter.

Silverback is up on all fours,
pacing back and forth,
his eyes never leaving Snub and Breath
as he punches the earth,
saying *Come sooner.*

As she slips and staggers forward,
Snub imagines the crocodile's jaws
locking on her leg,
she and Breath dragged under.

Silverback's strong arms pull Breath from her,
then return to drag Snub along a sodden trunk,
slide her over mossy wood,
and finally bring her to rest
on a broad, flat stone.

Hands are on Snub,
snagging in her clodded hair.

There is a lot of grooming to do.

Brother pulls half a crushed earthworm from between Snub's
     toes.
Teased sniffs globs of mud before rubbing them into the grass,
then flicks sodden weeds from Snub's back.

It is Silverback who grooms Snub's face,
smoothing out her wet hair,
his thumbs heavy as slumber against her forehead.

Snub closes her eyes and faces the ash-dimmed sun.

hoo!

Waking, the sun hot and bright.

Where is Breath?
Where is Mother?

Snub sits up, eyes open wide.

Brother is startled.
He jerks and rolls,
nearly pitching into the dark pond
before he catches himself and rights to all fours.
He glares at Snub.

Broken nettles are under Snub's back.
Someone made her a nest and placed her in it.

There is Mother!

She faces away from Snub, hunched and rocking.
The triangles of her shoulder blades jut,
her hair is even thinner than before.

Where is Breath?

Snub circles to see what is in Mother's arms.

Breath is there.
Dirty, but whole.

Latched to Mother,
filling himself.

Snub sits beside Mother and Breath,
feels the warmth of their bodies,
listens
to the slurping sound of alive.

A feeling of missing.
That is when Snub realizes it:
Wrinkled is gone.

Maybe Wrinkled will be back home,
whenever they finally get there.

Maybe Wrinkled will
be waiting for them
when they all arrive.

The flood took the family a long way.

The mountain that used to hold
the soft forest of home
is at the horizon,
no longer red but still spewing its clouds of dark gray.

At the far side of it
is a small arc of sky.
Blue!
Some of the sky is not gray.

Silverback's eyes cast toward home,
but his body faces the other way.

Snub knows that he means
to bring them into unknown places
instead of back toward the mountain.

But Snub wants to go home.

They must choose.
They cannot stay at the edge of this pond,
full of milling predators.

Snub has always been content to watch Silverback decide.
She has never tried to convince Silverback
of anything.

She moves so she's directly in front of Mother,
exaggerating each movement
so Mother can't help but notice her.
Mother's bones creak as
she follows Snub,
joining her in heading toward the fallen mountain,
toward home.

Brother follows Mother.
Teased follows Brother.
Silverback follows Teased.

That's how it happens.
Snub is leading them.

Snub!

The silverback who led the family
before Silverback
began to leave blood in his nests,
slowed down until one day
he headed into a forested canyon
and never returned.

The baby who would have been Brother
was still and blue beneath black.

A young female tumbled from a tree
on a warm, boring, sunny morning.
The family panicked at bone shards
poking through bloody flesh.
The female dragged herself away,
baring her teeth at any who tried to follow.

They died alone.
The family did not witness it.

Gorillas Snub has known have died,
but she has never seen one die.

Snub traces a narrow gully of exposed earth
away from the pond,
her family a line behind her,
placing their feet where hers have gone,
like ants do.

Black water runs
through the gully like a vein.
Ashy birds dot its surface,
acting less like birds and more like beetles,
too wet to fly and too nervous
to accept being stuck on the ground.
They hop in circles,
they hold their wings out to dry,
startling as the gorillas pass,
scattering on their spindly legs,
squawking.

Wrinkled is still gone.

Breath clutches Mother's belly,
his head peeking around
so he can watch Snub.
His eyes are heavy lidded,
his hair still caked with ash and mud,
but he stays awake and focused on her.
Snub purses her lips and makes the sounds of

acha.

Breath's eyes widen, and he purses his lips back.
He hasn't yet figured out how to make sounds,
but Snub gets the feeling of

acha

from the way he looks at her.
He sucks on his little finger.

Snub follows this gully
because the gully follows the cliff
and the cliff is what blocks them
from home.

The jungle spreads shade
over the gully,
over the gorillas.
The trees here have not fallen,
and tower high above the ground,
casting welcome darkness.

Roaches scurry between ferns.

Now that they are among trees
Silverback pauses them,
sniffing at the hollows of trunks
and ripping away planks of rotten bark.

The gorillas yank free
meaty chunks of softened wood,
dripping in mites,
and chew them as they go.

A crashing sound brings Snub
looking back for danger,
but Brother blocks her view,
gaping and unaware.

Since Brother is too dim
to keep them safe,
Snub moves to the rear.

Crash.

Snub peers for danger,
but there is only swaying green,
swelling clouds ever consuming the pale sun.

Crash.

Now Snub whirls in time to see their pursuers.

These are the two magpies,
the same that she once threw a nut at,
making more noise than their size should allow.
They are hopping around each other,
trying to get at whatever magpies like to get at
between blades of grass.

When the gorilla family moves forward,
the magpies follow.

Snub stares and stares at them.
In this strange new world,

magpies are following gorillas.
Maybe they think gorillas
will show them the way back home.

In this strange new world,
Snub's family is smaller by one
and bigger by two.

A night sky.

Snub is the only one awake,
her mind drifting from ash to heat
and drowned bodies.

Familiar pricks of light
poke through the black above,
same as they have always been.

The magpies sleep near,
right in the midst of Snub's family.
One has its eyes closed, head tucked under a wing,
while the other watches Snub warily.
Snub stares back into its hard black eye,
curious about these magpies
but unable
to know what they know.

The mountain that has fallen between
Snub's family and home
has no openings,
no canyons or passageways,
and though sunset is far off
they are all too tired to continue.

In times of

hoo,

Snub, like Brother, bedded
far from Silverback,
almost out of sight,
hands pinned between her thighs,
curious eyes turned to the world outside.

But today when Silverback makes his bedding-down sounds
in the middle of the gray, sun-starved afternoon,
lowers his body to its side in the singed yellow grass,
Brother plops down right beside him,
so he's cradled within his strong arms.

Silverback tugs Teased's trembling body closer,
so it, too, is within his reach.

Snub curls into the nook
at the backside of Silverback's knees.
She tugs Mother's body near,
wrapping arms and legs around it,
sensing that warmth is what shivering Mother

will need most to survive the early night.

Breath leaves Mother's nipple and works his way
over her frail shuddering ribs,
nestling himself in the cave
between Mother's back and Snub's chin.

The ground rumbles like a belly.

The huddle of gorilla is sweaty,
and the close air between their bodies
is full of the rot of upturned earth,
trapped under the smoky air above.

It is the smell of
worry,
but mainly it is the smell of
relief.

Silverback's back jerks,
yanking Snub from a deep sleep.

She fights to return to the dream world of old

hoo

but then she hears Silverback
crashing through the grass,
making his

wragh

and beating his chest.
Snub sits up, holds Breath tight to her,
Mother's hand in hers.
They listen and watch.

The half-moon
lights the meadow's edges,
but shows nothing of Silverback,
not even his gray-white hairs.

Wherever Silverback charges,
moongrass is carved out
and replaced by blackness.

Snub wonders what danger has set Silverback
to displaying like this.

Then:
yipping and yowling,
anxious and insistent.

Wild dogs.

The gorillas are being hunted.

Snub makes her own

wragh,

letting the dogs know,
wherever they are in the darkness,
that they have more than one gorilla to fight.

All the same, Snub thinks of
Teased and Mother and Breath,
easy meals for wild dogs,
and fear for them makes her go quiet.
She kicks out at Brother,
and the strong young gorilla
snorts and gets to his feet.
When Snub makes another

wragh,

Brother makes his own

wragh,

though since it's Brother
he probably hasn't figured out why.

The yips near and retreat,
become whines and worried barks.

Silverback is keeping himself
between the dogs and his family.

wragh!

He roars and a dog's yips
become a growling, slavering sound,

followed by a sharp gnashing of tooth striking tooth.
A grunt from Silverback.
A wet thud.
The whining stops.

Rustle.
A creature approaches, and Snub hopes it is
Brother or Silverback.
Not a dog.

Silverback makes one more
pap pap,
very near, and then his back is against Snub's.

Brother makes his own quieter
pap pap,
then settles in, too.

Snub somehow falls asleep,
but her dreams do not return to the old good feeling.
The future has come to be more important
than the past,
and the future does not bring
many feelings of

                                                    boo.

The magpies are rooting through the soil,
so used to Snub that one dances between her fingers
as it tries to get at a worm
pinned beneath Snub's hand.

The other is on top of Silverback's dozing body,
tucking an injured claw close to its underbelly
as it searches for ticks.

Lying on her side, head pillowed on her bicep,
Snub watches the wounded magpie watch her.

It tilts its head one way and then another,
like it is trying to communicate something.

Snub makes a quiet hoot back.
I see you.

The hoot has startled the magpies.
They fly in the direction of home.
Snub traces their path through the morning sky
and sees that the rockfall has an opening.
There is a canyon there
leading toward home
and that lick of blue sky.

The wounded magpie lands,
looks back at Snub

before hopping toward the canyon.
It looks back again.

I see you.

Again, Snub leads.

She is not at the front of the group,
but she stands beside Silverback,
holding a leaf between her lips,
staring into the canyon
for so long that Silverback cannot help
but understand what she thinks they should do.

A flash of black and white,
sharp against the greens and yellows of the grass,
as the magpie pair flies off into the canyon ahead.
They land in the upturned soil, inspecting the ground.
The magpie with the wounded leg looks at Snub,
head tilted quizzically,
then pecks out a bug and eats it.

The family approaches the canyon.
Air sloughs down from the mountains,
whistling and grumbling in Snub's ears.
It parts her hair, awakening the scrapes
and bruises along her skin.

They have reached the punctured edge of a new land.
The cliffs are an aged gray on the outside,
broken only by light green patches of moss and lichen.
The shattered inside of the canyon walls is
vibrant orange,
sharp and crumbling.

It looks like something that shouldn't be seen,
like the inside of a body,
and Snub hoots in sympathy.

Shards litter the ground.
Homeless bees swarm angrily around the rubble.

At the far side of the canyon,
blue sky in the direction of home.

Slowly,
pausing to sniff each orange boulder he passes,
Silverback climbs over the debris
and ventures into the canyon.

The family stays in a huddle
as they pick their way over the jagged terrain.
Canyon walls loom on either side,
framing a ribbon of cinder sky.

This is all Snub can see:
shards of orange rock beneath,
sandy sharp walls along either side,
teeming gray above.

Motes of ash drift down the narrow passage,
dusting the gorillas' hair in white gray,
making Silverback look like some other animal entirely
as he leads the way.

They come across nothing like food or shelter,
nothing that could ever produce

hoo.

But in the blue sky at the far end,
there is the promise that

hoo

might return someday.

Snub strokes Breath's back
and grooms trembling Mother
at the very sight of it.

PART THREE

OLD MEETS NEW

Skitter-scatter of rock
shards tumbling into the canyon,
sending the gorillas clutching one another—
except Silverback,
up on two legs and roaring.

Shapes line the ledge above.

Darting, grunting.
Maybe these are new gorillas.

Silverback beats his chest,

wragh.

Brother beats his chest,

wragh.

There are three of the creatures
looking down from the lip of the ridge.
They look almost like gorillas,
but if these are gorillas
their hair rubbed off somewhere,
and they are standing on two legs
for a very long time.
It must make their hips ache,
like Snub's did the night she spent in the dark pond.

These maybe-gorillas are excited,
shuffling positions to better peer at Snub's family.

Their hoots raise Snub's hair,
the pitch higher and louder than a gorilla's,
and changing within each breath.

The not-gorillas are running now,
making their strange calls,
pounding the ground.
Where once were three now are four.

Even though Silverback is on his back legs and
making his most ferocious

wragh,

these not-gorillas do not run away
but come toward Snub's family.

Their arrival sends loose stones tumbling.
Snub's family cowers,
arms over their heads.
Snub shelters Mother and Breath as best she can.

The not-gorillas make their jabbering calls,
kicking more stones down onto the family.
Silverback roars in outrage,
tries to climb the cliff face,
only making it a few feet
before he falls back,
clattering gravel.

With an especially loud jabbering shriek,
one of the not-gorillas picks up
a large rock in its two hands.
Its body becomes a straight line from fingertips to toes,

something Snub has never seen a gorilla do.

For a moment the not-gorilla is motionless,
silhouetted against the pale sun,
rock in its hands.

Then it casts it into the canyon.

The gorillas are stilled by the horror of it,
one creature throwing a rock at another.
Tumbling end over end,
the rock slams into the ground,
sending up a spray of shards,
then rolls away.

Snub shakes her fists at the not-gorillas
before coming back to the ground,
beating her chest, making a string of

wragh

and

mrgh

as ferocious as any Silverback ever made.

The not-gorillas are motionless,
staring down at them.

Snub whirls in confusion,
now aware of the chaos of sound around her.
The gorillas' cries echo,
combining and layering in the narrow canyon walls.
The not-gorillas are making their own cries, too:
excitement

lust
hunger.

One of the not-gorillas has another rock in its hands,
is once again silhouetted against the sun.
It sends it bouncing against the canyon walls,
slamming the sides,
fragmenting into a hail of smaller stones.

Snub protects Mother and Breath with her body.
Mother is beyond

wragh,

weakened by the journey,
quieted by shock.
Breath is motionless against her breast,
suckling for comfort.

Snub wants to race away,
but Silverback is holding his ground,
screaming his

wragh

at these not-gorillas.

Surely as it feels like waiting
for the next pitched rock
means waiting for death,
it also feels like
leaving the protection of Silverback
is even more certain death.

So Snub stays, roaring her

mrgh

up at the not-gorillas
even as one of them readies another rock.

While Silverback roars his loudest threat yet,
Snub again braces herself over Mother,
hoping her body can save Mother,
and that both their bodies can save Breath.

The rock does not fall.

Instead, Snub sees
the strange creatures back away
from the canyon's edge,
soon out of view,
vanishing like mist.

Silverback lets out a proud, defiant

wragh.

As the sound fades,
it reveals beneath it another sound,
one that has started to become almost familiar,
even as it sets Snub's spine straight and her muscles tight.

Yips.

The dogs look pathetic, famished, powerful, mean.
They must be why the not-gorillas left.

Long ago, Snub watched dogs worry down an antelope,
chasing it until it fell into the grass, exhausted,
then eating it without killing it first.
Now she watches them lope into the canyon,
one taking the lead for only a few moments before
cringing to the back of the pack,
tail low between its legs.

Silverback charges the first dog, his

wragh

sending it howling back to its pack.

A new dog tries, this one with a ragged ear standing up
and the other flopping down.
Behind it are more dogs than Snub has toes,
enough dogs to block the canyon
from one side to the other.

Snub wonders why they are coming near at all,
when Silverback is there to defend.

Silverback yawns widely and slowly
so each dog gets a good view of his long teeth.

Teased pulls herself past Snub and Brother and Mother and
    Silverback

so that she's the farthest along the canyon,
leaning heavily against the wall, gasping.

Brother runs tight back-and-forths behind Silverback,
kicking at rocks to add to his ruckus,
though they strike Silverback and not the enemies.

The dogs in the back press against the dogs in the front.
Without courage, the whining, snarling pack
creeps steadily closer to Silverback.

Silverback's fear-scent is thickened
by the close canyon walls,
enough to make Snub gag.
Breath whimpers with fright,
switching to Snub's belly from Mother's.

One of the dogs, yowling as if it has already been attacked,
tries to creep past Silverback.
Its eyes are on Snub—or actually, she realizes,
its eyes are on Breath.

Holding tight to the baby,
Snub backs down the canyon,
huddling with Mother.

No dog will eat Breath while Snub is still alive
to protect him.

Silverback lunges at the dog and it leaps away,
the gorilla's meaty fist slamming into rocky ground.

The pack retreats, but only for a moment,
again pressing forward, another dog in the lead,
this one all black with a single tan burst on one ear.

Silverback leaps right where the dog tries to escape.
His fist cracks its back.

Silverback bounds back to the center of the canyon,
leaving the dog's halves to thrash.
    Its eyes are panicky, tongue lolling,
        front and back legs moving at different speeds.

The dogs hassle forward.
Brother springs into motion, clubbing at a dog.
His fist hits its snout,
but the dog is barely injured,
whirls and sinks its teeth into Brother's forearm.
He punches out, sending the dog flying back into its pack.

Another dog feints forward,
and again Silverback leaps to fend it off,
leaving the far side of the canyon unguarded.

Brother lets the dog creep past him.
It circles Snub and Mother. Breath.

The baby is terrified,
little fingers digging into Snub's ribs.
She would fight the dogs if she were on her own,
but the need to protect Breath
makes her want

only to run and flee,
whatever will let the baby survive.

She hears the cries of gorillas and the squeals of dogs.
The close rock walls make everything echo
so that she is unsure who is in pain or where.

Mother is alive.
She is beside Snub,
cowering against the canyon wall.

Brother and Silverback are fighting off the pack.
Together they block enough of the canyon
that no more dogs can stream through.

Snub can still hear the sounds of a gorilla in pain.
She cocks her head at the echo,
only slowly realizing that there are new cries fueling it,
that a gorilla is still being attacked,
that this pain is new and continuing.

It is Teased.
The dogs have come from both ends of the canyon.
While most of them are harrying and distracting Silverback,
a pair has sneaked down the other side of the canyon
and set upon Teased.

They are pulling and tearing at flesh and skin.
Teased is not moving, not anymore.
Her cries have stopped.
Teased has stopped.

Snub has seen the dogs
stop Teased.

Fear heats up.
Fear becomes something blinding.
Snub cries out her

mrgh

at the dogs and strikes her chest in rage
until her vision returns.

Silverback turns toward her,
charges toward the pair of dogs to send them
howling and scattering from Teased
    or what, Snub sees now, once was Teased and now is
    leg, tissue, skin without Teased to combine them,
    the inside of her facing out.

Silverback roars right next to Snub,

mrgh

in his voice and also pain.

Brother and Mother have thronged to his side,
while he
    whirls and circles,
    whirls and circles,
fists whaling at dogs.

Clutching Breath,
Snub steals to the shelter of Silverback's body.
A dog has slinked back to Teased's corpse,
its snout stained red, whining all the while.
Silverback makes sounds of

mrgh,
wragh,

charging the dog and sending it fleeing.

It is not fast enough.
Silverback's jaws are around its neck.
After one quick and ferocious bite,
the dog's body jerks uselessly on the ground.

Silverback charges down the canyon,
racing heedlessly toward the patch of blue sky,
toward distant home,
dashing wild dogs with wide sweeps of his arms,
his breath so ragged and choppy
that Snub can track him by sound alone.
Brother follows him.

Snub takes Mother's hand,
brings her bobbing and hobbling down the canyon.
Mother makes gurgling confused noises as she goes.

The canyon whips past
as they follow Silverback.
The dogs' excited cries fade, turning to
snarls as they tear at the body that used to be Teased.
The

mrgh

of it makes Snub run faster.
Though part of her wants to whirl and attack,
to release the feeling,
to kill a dog,
she is stopped by her

for the baby clinging to her ribs.

Silverback slows his charge,
watching over his shoulder
to be sure the dogs aren't following.

Snub is glad to give Mother the chance to recover.
The sharp rocks of the canyon have scraped her limbs.
Whimpering, Breath moves from Snub back to Mother,
holding himself tight to her chest and beginning to feed.
Snub would like nothing more than to lay out flat
on the rocky floor of the crevasse
and rest,
but Silverback won't let them stop.
Panting and stumbling,
vision blurring and feet numbing,
Snub follows Brother and Silverback
along the rock-strewn floor.

Though most of the canyon wall
is tall and unbroken,
the gorillas pass a fallen-in spot where a rockslide
has formed a steep slope up to the top.

A pair of dog pups appears at the edge,
staring down at the gorillas,
mouths opening and closing,
as if unsure whether to make any noise.
A mother dog is behind them, whining,
nipples swollen.
She nuzzles her pups out of view.

Silverback picks up speed.
Snub is following, but her mind
is on Teased,
on the parts of Teased
that are meant to be
inside Teased.
It is all Snub can do to keep her limbs moving
under the hot and constant sun.

Finally
the sharp, rocky ground slopes.
The canyon walls open out.
Ahead the earth is not broken.
The land beyond the canyon is
green,
slopes intersecting in fogged ravines,

all of it covered by trees and vines,
flecked with bright chattering birds.

Mist flows through,
shrouding the trunks and hills,
until it parts in the distance to reveal
a waterfall
as tall as the tallest tree,
its flow sparkling
into a lagoon of gray stone
whose glistening surface twinkles the light.

This is not home.
But could it become home?

The familiar foods of their old homeland
grow here, too:
a cluster of red figs at the summit of a palm,
nettles sprouting from the cracks of a rotting trunk,
ponderous fronds shaped like elephant ears
that will taste bitter until Snub bites into the stalk
and the sweetness inside makes the mouthful soft.

Though her body is still jangly with exhaustion
after the flight from the dogs,
Snub senses that maybe,
even though her family has lost
Wrinkled and Teased,
they could all come to feel

hoo

again here.

Black lines draw themselves across the sky,
and Snub looks up to see the two magpies soaring past,
coasting the currents
rising over the sheer green slope.
They land on the glossy smooth stones
at the edge of the lagoon.

Snub is the only one still on the orange canyon rock.
Forward, the swell of clean blue sky,
the promise of safety
and of future

boo.

Snub looks back one last time.

Though nothing is moving in the canyon,
teeming ash and smoke in the background
make the passage of broken rock
appear simultaneously to grow and shrink,
the air itself crawling.

Snub finds motion in it,
and not just the tricks of the air.

There.
Almost invisible at the canyon's horizon,
she can make out the tips of the dogs' ears.

They think they are hiding,
but they are not.

One of their ears pivots and then goes still,
cupped in the direction of Snub's family.

The dogs are intent on the gorillas,
want to eat the gorillas,
but they dare not follow them into the new green area.

Snub is confused.
The dogs were brave enough to attack even Silverback.
What are they scared of now?

Snub is glad for the lagoon.
The sound of the waterfall tumbling.

hoo.

Time passes
without gorillas noticing that
time passes.

Here are vines with spicy leaves
that make Snub's tongue tingle.

Here are macaws, parakeets,
and always the pair of magpies.

Here wounds heal,
become scars and not scabs.

Though Snub is careful to stay
within sight of Mother and Breath,
she once again might go the whole day
without seeing Silverback or Brother
until it is the time to make night nests.

Snub and Mother pass their fingers
through each other's hair
whenever they are next to each other,
searching for worms or ticks but really saying
We are alive together.

Whenever Mother lies down to rest—
which happens more and more often
as dry season becomes wet season becomes dry—
Breath tucks himself onto her belly,
clutching her hard,
desperate for warmth within the swelter of midday.
When Mother's naps go long
he journeys off along the jungle floor,

often placing his face right beside Snub's,
studying the plants Snub eats,
taking his own tiny handfuls of whatever Snub tastes,
chomping gustily with his tiny teeth.

Breath has stopped attaching himself to Mother's breast.
Even when Snub is cross with him,
when Breath has set on her with his tweaking pinches
or his impish punches,
she never thinks of him as the pink worm anymore.

This young gorilla has sprouted a mop of thick hair on his head,
a particularly big reddish curl rising
in a wave,
like the licks of water that taste the edge of the lagoon.

Snub gets distracted
and sits on Brother.

She had been picking through a thatch of ferns
for the youngest and springiest fiddleheads
and didn't notice him behind her.

Snub realizes that they have not played
their falling-into-each-other game
in a long time.

Maybe it is because
ever since the canyon,
the fight with the dogs,
the seasons at the lagoon,
Brother doesn't play.
He doesn't lag behind the world anymore,
because he is behind Silverback.
Wherever Silverback goes,
Brother goes, too,
even though his back isn't at all silver.

No one else seems to care that this is not home.

They forage at this nut tree like it is the same
as the nut tree that grew between the two rocks.
They eat these green spaded leaves like they are the same
as the green spaded leaves of Teased's favorite fern.

But Snub has memories of another, better place.
Every day, she seeks out the limits of her world,
hoping to find a sign of which way is home.
She travels far over the jungle floor,
as far as the clay-brown river
or the orange cliffs of the canyon.
She runs until she is exhausted,
until she has rushed far from the lagoon,
along the clay-brown river,
through the reeds at the bank,
scattering the columns of flies skimming the edge.
She collapses into a patch of soft wildflowers,
chest heaving and arms trembling,
calmness stolen by longing.

The sky and the flowers eventually relax her,
and she places her arms behind her head,
lets her thoughts unfocus as she stares at the clouds.

The magpies are near, following her as always,
pretending not to be aware of her

as they pick seeds out from between the wildflowers.

Maybe they remember home.

Maybe Snub's family is the last piece of it they can find.

Snub follows the clay-brown river
away from the lagoon,
farther than she ever has,
hoping for clues of home.

It threads through the jungle,
overhung by spindly trees
that drape lichen,
that host parakeets and monkeys.

Snub follows the river until it disappears
into marshy ground,
turning into still water blanketed in mosquitoes
that mire in Snub's coarse hair.

Snub has seen rivers flow into lakes and ponds,
but never slowly weaken and disappear like this,
like they are dying,
like the ground is a dry dog
ripping and biting the river
until it is gone.
The sight takes away Snub's flimsy feeling of

hoo.

Did she hear voices?
Snub whirls on thickets of reeds,
glaring into each one.

Courage breaks, and Snub speeds
back toward Silverback.

She's already at the lagoon
before she remembers herself and stops.
She turns around despite the fear inside her,
but realizes that the day is too old
to go back exploring.

Snub takes a long look at her family.
Mother is asleep, her back rising and falling.
Breath has just woken, belly-down on top of Mother.
He props himself up on his elbows,
the better to watch Snub.

There's a look of sleepy outrage on his face,
as if he's unsure of what sound he should make,
confusion or sorrow or anger
at the fact that Snub has been wandering again.

The sky is dropping rain today.
The clouds bleach the sky
to an even, glowing white,
brightening the greens below.

The ash clouds did the same thing,
and the shift in the jungle's color
adds an edge to Snub's adventure,
makes her nervous and watchful.

She looks down the clay-brown river,
where there comes a sound,
a distant, regular thud.
like a tree releasing fruit.
Drum, drum, drum.
Snub has never heard any sound as regular as this before.

When the river dissolves into swamp,
gurgling away into muddy reeds,
the drumming stops.

Snub is left with only the noise of
mosquitoes batting her ears.

Careful as she tries to be, Snub slurps muck
with each step.

Spooked by her own noise, she climbs a tree.

Now that she is up high,
she can see farther.
Now that she can see farther,
she hoots in astonishment.

After the swamp ends, the trees thin out.
Tall yellow grasses sway in hot breeze,
steaming as rainwater rises into the sky.

There, at the base of a nearby tree,
is one of the not-gorillas.

This creature looks like a skinny naked gorilla.
It is longer than Snub is, much longer,
and though its hair is the same black,
it's as thin as the pink worm's before he became
Breath with his thick curl.
Its two ears are almost stubs,
as if the weird and hapless thing
got them caught somewhere
and had to bite them off.

It is faced away, hunched over some work in its lap,
making rhythmic repetitive motions
like a gorilla removing stubborn bark from a shoot of bamboo.

Because being still means feeling safe,
Snub keeps as still as she can.
The not-gorilla wipes its forehead,
turning slightly as it does.
Snub can see its face.

What a wretched and ugly thing!
Its nose sticks far out before retreating

to a mouth that is weak and narrow,
a mouth that couldn't contain teeth
that are strong or long—
or maybe it doesn't have teeth at all.
Its hair is sparse,
leaving skin exposed to stinging vines and insect bites.

As she stares at the not-gorilla,
Snub feels less fear and more pity.
How can a creature as frail as this survive?

At first she thinks it is a bushbuck on the not-gorilla's lap,
but then she realizes it's only the skin of a bushbuck,
that the animal has left its fur behind.

On top of the skin is a heavy blunt stone.
The not-gorilla has another rock in its fist,
which it raises up high and brings crashing down.
Smash.
A fleck chips off the stone, which is becoming
sharper.
The creature examines that stone,
holding it close to its eyes, testing the edge
on its cheek.

Its—his—look is almost tender, almost prideful.
Like how Mother looks at Breath.
Snub hoots softly in wonder,
realizing she can see in the not-gorilla's expression
feelings that gorillas have, too.

The not-gorilla stands,
showing that he's even skinnier
than Snub first thought.
Maybe this one is sick.

He walks along the grassland's edge,
the sharpened rock in his fist.

He twirls, raising and lowering the rock in his hand, strutting
like Brother does when he's following Silverback.
Then the not-gorilla stops unexpectedly,
raises the sharp rock as high in the air as he can,
makes weird gibbering sounds, and brings the rock crashing
into a tree trunk,
breaking it in two and spraying chips.

Snub nearly falls from her perch,
she is so astonished.
When she looks back at the not-gorilla,
he is staring right at her.

For a moment they lock eyes.
Snub's stomach falls away.
Looking at him is looking into the eyes of a
dream creature that has chased her
into the waking world.

The not-gorilla seems shocked, too.
His jaw hangs open.

Then he's yelling and twirling his rock,
and Snub makes a

wragh

that is only about fear,
empty of

mrgh.

She races through the brush,
hoots her terror as loudly as she can

in the hope that Silverback will hear her,
that he will come save her.

There are more cries behind her,
more strange calls of the not-gorillas.
It's not just her crashing through the brush,
not anymore.

Snub imagines the sharpened stone
slamming into her
like how it shattered the tree,
jagged like the hot rocks the mountain
once sent after them.

She tries to follow the clay-brown river's course
without leaving the cover of the trees,
but at one spot a muddy patch of earth
gives way.

Snub lands in the water:
shock of the cold
feeling of quick drowning
a memory of a terrifying night
once spent in the middle of a dark new pond.
Snub's body hurls itself out at the far bank,
her mind whiplashing after it.

She crashes headlong into the brush,
still hearing the not-gorilla cries,
distant but insistent,
the drumming sound is back,
now she's lost

on the wrong side of the lagoon,
maybe she's heading toward the dogs
or the not-gorillas,
but staying still is not an option,
not with her heart racing
her limbs quivering
her body releasing everything that's inside of her
all over the green-swept earth.

Her panicked cries silence some birds.
Others it sends into raucous flights,
handfuls of color sprinkling the sky.

When she can run no longer,
Snub buries herself in a thicket,
heedless of the winged ants crawling over her,
knowing only that she feels safer to be hidden,
even if being hidden also means being bitten.

Snub smells her own dung,
the dung her fear has produced.
It tells her of home and her family,
of how much she wants to be back.

Staying motionless is easy,
but the feelings that come from being motionless
are hard.
Snub watches for not-gorillas,
every turning leaf
and creaking branch
draining what energy she has left.

Knowing that at least a gorilla asleep alone
is safer
than a gorilla wandering about alone,
Snub can't help but shut her eyes.

Snub wakes to yellow eyes
in a green spade head.

The snake is as large as the world
until Snub recoils,
until she realizes how small the snake is
and reaches for it,
has it running over her fingers
before it escapes into the brush.

Behind the snake are the two magpies.
One hops near,
pecks a plump winged ant off Snub's arm hair.
The other joins it,
and Snub watches in wonder as
together
they eat the ants that were crawling on her.

She knows they are trying to fill their bellies,
but it feels like they are grooming her,
like a gorilla would.
It brings a strange

boo.

Screams nearby, and coming closer.

wragh.

The tendrils of a willow shake,
and then through its leaves
erupts one of the not-gorillas.

When it sees Snub
it tries to turn around
but only trips,
splaying out in the dirt.
Silverback
bursts into the
clearing right
after it.
He is as surprised
as the not-gorilla
to find Snub there.
His heel smashes into
its gut, then
Silverback slams into Snub,
bloodying her mouth,
hurling her
into the dirt.

Silverback charges after the not-gorilla,
leaving Snub staggered and alone,
with only the caws of the magpies
and Silverback's pungent fear-odor.

Then Brother is there, too.
His eyes are wide in fear.
He's spraying dung as he goes.
He sees Snub and skids to a stop,
blinks at her in confusion,
then goes off to follow Silverback.

Snub races after Brother.
Until a sound stops her.

Mother.

Snub parts the willow leaves.
They have been softening Mother's sound;
it's easier to make out the feeling now,
the pained gasps and whimpers.

Mother is curled in the soil,
head tilted and neck cranked.
The part of her face
above the nose and below the brows
is a mess of red-black-brown.
Mother's knees are flat
and her hips are high.

Despite Mother's continuing cries
Snub thinks she must be dead,
that no gorilla who was alive would ever
sit on the earth this way.

Mother wrenches her head up
as Snub approaches, but her face
points only vaguely in Snub's direction.
A little black creature emerges
from under her,
toddles toward Snub.

Mother was in that strange position
because she was protecting Breath.

Breath is
squealing
agitated
baffled
bloodied.

When Snub steps toward him
he runs back to Mother.
He's soon up around her neck,
striking her cheeks with his palms,
trying to give her motion.
But though Mother's limbs may tremble,
She cannot seem to get up.

Snub comes close to Mother,
leans beside her,
frantically grooms
her bloodied hair.

Mother rests her head in Snub's hand.
It is heavy.

Mother's mouth is gaping open.
Without quite knowing why
Snub runs her fingers over Mother's teeth,
feeling them, memorizing their touch.

Excited cries from not-gorillas nearby.
Mother's body seizes.
She's frantic,
arms flailing in the dirt.

Snub thinks she's trying to get to her hands and feet,
but instead Mother's arms are around Breath,
clutching him clumsily and roughly,
making Breath cry out in pain and bite at her fingers
until she holds him out to Snub.
    You must take him.
    I will die here.

Snub realizes what Mother wants.
She backs away in terror,
but Mother is holding out Breath,
shaking him,
making him cry in fear and nip at her arms to get down.

Snub hears the cries of the not-gorillas as they race nearer,
and that terrible drumming.

Snub remembers the sight of
Silverback's desperate rage
and Brother's fear
and the weight of
what she must do
blows her back.

Snub takes the squirming
gorilla child into her arms.
He clutches tight to her,
head buried in her chest.

Snub backs toward the willow leaves,
toward the noises of Silverback.

She makes sounds of

acha

for Mother to hear
instead of the drumming.

Even as she crashes through fronds and branches,
away from the not-gorillas,
Snub sees only the last sight of Mother,
rickety arms crossed over her chest.

Snub would have stayed with her
if Mother hadn't given her Breath to care for.
You must take him.
I will die here.

Snub holds Breath close and runs,
keeps her mind on the warm jiggling life
in her arms,
races over trunks and thickets
and nets of vines.
Breath is quiet against her chest.
Snub knows from the cheek against her breastbone
that he is staring back after Mother.

Silverback's pungent fear-scent leads Snub
to the edge of the lagoon's river,
where it vanishes.
A gash has been ripped into the foliage at the far bank,
a fresh tan oval of mud where a large stone
has tumbled into the water.

Snub picks her way across,
Breath shifting up to her shoulders,

arms slapped across her forehead,
fingers anchored in her ears.

At the far bank she finally stills.
She allows herself
a moment to live
in the memory of Mother.

Snub finds Silverback and Brother in day nests,
splayed out and panting.
Silverback has a gash on the high crown of his head.
Brother cradles one hand in the other,
whimpering while he massages his palm.

Snub sits between the two males.
Breath gets down from her head
and settles into her lap,
making confused hoots.
He walks a few lengths away,
one direction and then another,
pleading.

He is looking for Mother.

Breath lifts Silverback's giant hand,
looks beneath it for Mother.

Silverback, startled out of his sleep,
grunts in

amrcha

and cuffs Breath, sending him
sprawling into the dirt.

Breath surprises Snub by making a grunt of

amrcha

back.

Snub runs forward, cringing, and scoops up Breath,
retreating with him to the other side of the clearing.
Breath fights mightily in her arms,
jumps down,
breaks sticks,
thumps trunks.
Snub races after him,
trying to get him back into her arms.

This work,
this wrangling of Breath,
seems like the only way to
move against the heavy sight
of Mother wounded,
of Mother dead,
of dying Mother left by Snub.

This work is also the reason
Snub can't go back to her.
Breath keeps Snub
from endangering Snub.

Finally Breath's tantrum hurls him into the dirt,
fists pummeling soil.
Snub wrenches him roughly up,
hunches her body over the child.
She accepts his bites and scratches,
deserves his bites and scratches,
muffles his grunts
in the coarse, thick hair of her belly.

Gradually he shudders into silence.
Snub folds over his little heaving body,
feels his gasps wetting her hair.

Snub's thoughts are on Mother
in a clearing far away,
or no longer in a clearing.
Mother gone.

A long time without feeding,
without moving at all.

Snub spies a bracket fungus
growing from a stump.
A gorilla would have to be in
this very nest,
in this very position
to see it.

She fills her mouth with its woody, tooth-squeaking flesh.
As she's chewing and swallowing she is aware of her teeth.
She thinks of Mother's, of the touch of them under her
     fingertips.

Snub's eating slows,
she lowers her hands
to her lap,
stares dazedly off.

She has been fighting for

hoo,

but

hoo

cannot come from fighting.

Breath is facedown in Snub's nest,
curled over himself,
fists tight and eyes scrunched.
He's gotten rheumy during the night.
His sleep breathing is wheezy and wet.

Snub lies down next to Breath.
She runs a finger along his thumb,
tugs it free of the tensed fingers,
picks through the red curl
on top of his head,
marveling at his body.

Breath has no scars.
That was Mother's work.

Snub hears bees, follows the noise and returns
with a molten glob of honeycomb,
dripping yellow onto dark green.
It is for Breath.
It is what Mother would have given Breath.

Before Snub can feed it to him,
Silverback looms over Snub,
breathing out heavily,
his throat in the shape of

wragh

so that,
even though he isn't making his intimidating bark,
fear quickens Snub's pulse.

Snub will not give up this honeycomb.

She gutters air out her nose,
holding perfectly still,
avoiding Silverback's gaze
until he grunts in irritation and charges away,
pretending there is an enemy that needs scaring.

Snub waves the honeycomb under Breath's nose.
He moans and jerks awake.
Leaning back against Snub,
he lazily accepts the piece,
staring into Snub's eyes as he groggily

chews it and swallows it down,
honey matting the hair of his chin.

Snub offers him another piece.
When he bites it this time,
something changes inside Breath.
He squeals, nips Snub on the knuckle,
runs across the clearing, shrieking away.

The last piece of honeycomb has fallen into the dirt.

Brother picks it up and eats it,
though it is covered in leaves and mud.

Breath runs from Snub all morning,
kicking at trees, rocks, the magpies.

Snub does not mind.
The work of following Breath
keeps her own thoughts away from Mother,
from the sorrow that is Snub's version
of Breath's anger.

Sometimes Breath will stop what he's doing
and stare off into the distance,
always in the same direction,
always toward the place
where Mother pressed him into Snub's arms.

> *You must take him.*
> *I will die here.*

When the sun is at its highest
it makes its own trees of light,
glistening mote-filled trunks
of empty brightness
between the dark-leafed spaces of the jungle.

Snub wakes to orange-brown valleys of aging light.

Brother is investigating a termite mound,
his lips smacking loudly as he tries to chew down
muscled termite guards before they can bite his lips.
His moans and whimpers make Snub think
Brother and the termites are evenly matched.

Silverback is still asleep.
Without his pool of sunshine he must have gotten cold.
He has dragged fronds over his broad back.

Snub reaches her arms tighter around Breath.
But there is no Breath.

She darts to all fours, turns circles,
grunts out her worry and

                                         acha.

Breath isn't anywhere.

A branch is broken,
dripping white sap onto the sodden ground.
Snub heads that way,
holding out a finger to capture some of the sweet, tangy fluid,
bringing it to her mouth as she goes.

Without quite expecting it,
Snub is back in the clearing
beneath the willow leaves.

The grass is still bent where once was Mother.
Snub's heart pounds with the loss of her,
but riding above that feeling,
insistent,
is her worry about Breath.

He is not here.
Snub makes a quick *pap pap* on her chest,
like she once did
when she hoped Silverback would rescue her.
But now she is hoping to be the one to rescue.

Far off, a response.
The cry of a young gorilla.

Snub wants to race headlong toward Breath,
but here
the not-gorillas could be nearby.

She creeps as quietly as she can,
wincing when a vine turns out to be
brittle,
crackling under her toes,
or a pile of leaves hides a hole
that makes her grunt in surprise.

On the far side of a muddy puddle
teeming with water striders,
Snub finally spies Breath.

He is at the edge of the jungle,
staring into the open grassland
where Snub once spied a not-gorilla
making a dull stone
into a sharp stone.

Waves of yellow-green grasses
shake and flatten
with every shift of the winds.

Breath totters on two legs,
hopping as he tries get a view over the tall grass.

The not-gorillas are there.

There are more not-gorillas than Snub has fingers.

The carcass of a boar hangs from a wood frame,
legs splayed, hide peeled partially away,
the edges where meat joins skin
dripping runny red-brown juice into the grass.

One of the not-gorillas is hacking into the corpse
with a sharpened stone,
the soft thin hair along its body
matted with sweat.
Another, much smaller one
is watching, hefting a rock of its own.

Other not-gorillas are in poses that a gorilla might make:
lounging together,
examining a nutshell for any morsel left inside,
grunting.
There is so much to watch.
Snub can understand why Breath is looking out at them
with such wonder.

None of the not-gorillas has seen him,
but they will soon.
Grunting as loudly as she dares,
Snub creeps through the grass,
stopping right behind Breath,
snaking out a finger
to flick the tuft of white hair on his rump.

He squeaks in joy,
falls into Snub's arms,
trembling with fear
or relief from fear.

The not-gorillas raise their strange voices,
the dry grass
swishing
rasping
along with them.

Snub and then Breath wriggle on their bellies
back into the cover of the jungle.

As Snub gets to all fours and begins to speed
back toward Silverback,
Breath bites her hand.
He toddles back toward the not-gorillas,
pausing at the edge of the jungle to watch them.

If she pulls him away,
he will shriek and reveal them both.

Chest heaving, Snub curls beside Breath,
her arm around his tender belly,
waiting for him
to want to leave
the creatures that attacked Mother.

A female not-gorilla has a child
that is Breath's size,
but unlike Breath this child
does not hold on to its mother.

Useless child.
The mother must use one arm
to keep it on her hip
while she roots in the soil with the other.
Every time the not-gorilla mother leans forward,
the child dips to the earth,
squalling as its head lolls.

Three males sit in the tall grass.

One is watchful,
looking toward the more distant grassland,
where Snub can see a small-eared elephant.
Short trunk, downward tusks.

The not-gorilla is intent on it,
fingers clenching and unclenching
a large animal bone at its side,
as if to strike out with it.

Strange.
Though it is excited, the not-gorilla
makes no sounds out of its feelings,
is being completely quiet.

That elephant is so large.
The not-gorillas can pose no threat to it.

The other two males are standing on two legs.
Why does it not cause them pain to stand for so long?

The female grubbing in the dirt
pulls out a root,
clods of earth raining from it,
plinking into the grass.

Snub has never considered this,
digging food out of the ground,
but recognizes the eating pleasure
of the female not-gorilla.

The tuber makes a satisfying crack
when the female bites into it,
like bamboo.
Snub imagines it in her own mouth,
crisp and watery.

One of the males hears the cracking sound, too.
He knocks the tuber from the female's hands,
picks it up from the dirt,
tears into woody flesh with strong jaws.

Breath watches the not-gorillas.
He thrusts his shoulder into Snub,
leaning hard into her belly,
so hard it hurts.
His fingers twist into the hair on her legs and pull,
and she scrunches her eyes at the pain.
Then his hands finally relax.
Breath goes limp.

He will let them leave now.

Snub holds him tight to her and turns around,
picking her way into the jungle on all fours.
When she takes one last look back,
she sees a not-gorilla child has noticed them.
This one is older, closer to Snub's size than Breath's.

This child does not raise the alarm.
She does not let the others know.

Her arms are slack by her side,
wonder is on her face at the sight
of something as ordinary
as a pair of gorillas.

That not-gorilla child looked at Snub.
Even more than that—she *saw* Snub.
As she and Breath escape into the jungle,
Snub glances back, afraid to see
the child following, part of her
hoping to see the child following.
The only movements she sees, though,
are vines and leaves set springing
by Snub and Breath's passage.

Back in the clearing,
back with Silverback and Brother,
time slows again.
Snub forces herself not to think
about the not-gorillas.

A patch of greens drenched in sunlight.
Is there any better place for a gorilla to be?

hoo?

Breath is not satisfied.

Snub recognizes the mischief in his face
but cannot stop him before he has
plopped in between Silverback and his food.

While Silverback eats,
Breath wallops him on the wrist,
then sprints away,
wailing in terror.

Brother staggers out of the way
as Silverback charges after Breath.
Snub tries to place herself between them,
but Silverback

wragh

knocks Breath to the jungle floor,
rolling and biting him,
Breath crying.

When Silverback releases him,
Breath limps away before
tumbling on his wounded leg.

Snub tries to groom away Breath's pain,
but it stays until the next morning.

Breath spends that day at Snub's side,
avoiding Silverback,
his body always touching Snub's somewhere.

Home.

Here at the lagoon,
where there is green life
and blue water,
it is harder to remember
what felt so good about
her old home that
Snub was willing to risk everything
to get back there.

Home.

It used to exist
in the feeling of Silverback,
but with Mother gone
and Breath ever near,
home
is a feeling of keeping him safe
instead of a feeling
of being kept safe.

Snub cannot keep her hands on Breath always,
because then she would not eat or groom.

Breath is calm
for long stretches of the day,
and then he takes off,
and by the time Snub finds him
he is already watching
the not-gorillas,
drawn to the animals
that attacked Mother
as if watching them
will help him figure out
where Mother has gone.

Though the not-gorillas terrify Snub,
Breath will shriek if she tries
to drag him away early,
so she watches with him
until he tires.

Snub learns they like to pile bones.
They like to sleep on the skins of dead animals.
They sometimes howl and chant,
moving in ragged formations.
The drumming that Snub once heard was from
elephant skulls that they beat
with elephant bones.

After the drumming, blood mats their thin hair.
Great clots of it dangle from their mouths,
some of it still attached to meat.
Snub understands it is not their blood covering them
but some other animal's.

No gorilla would eat an animal this way.
No monkey would eat an animal this way.
The not-gorillas eat like lions and hyenas do.

A fight.

Silverback and Brother run away from
the sounds of it,
but Breath runs toward it.
Maybe he hopes now the not-gorillas
will answer
the question
of Mother.

Snub follows Breath, and they watch
from the jungle cover as a new family
of not-gorillas uses the bones
of dead animals to attack the not-gorillas
that Breath and Snub have come to know.

One with silver hair grips a tusk in both hands
and swings it around,
knocking a male flat on his side.

The female who dug up the tuber
comes to the male's defense,
throwing herself in front of his body,
and the silver-haired not-gorilla
turns the tusk on her instead.

Her child,
the one who saw Snub,
is a few feet away,

hands at her side,
wailing.

Breath is stirred,
making his sad hoots
as he tries to get out of Snub's lap.

None of the other not-gorillas
dare come to the defense
of the pair being smashed into the ground.
They cast their hands and feet above them,
trying to fend off the blows.
Anguished cries become
gurgling cries, then those, too, eventually stop.

The silver-haired not-gorilla wrenches
the tusk out of the bodies on the ground,
points it at a giant rock in the distance,
makes one of their strange high-pitched utterances,
and begins to walk.
The others shuffle along with him,
picking up their animal skins and rocks as they go.
The tiniest not-gorillas are scooped into the arms of females.
The rest of the young are led by the hand.

The small wailing child has been rooted
ever since the attack started.
Once the silver-haired not-gorilla is far away,
she throws herself into the grass
with the bodies of the dead.

Over time
the child's wails muffle.

She sits up,
hair streaked with the liquid leaking from her eyes,
and continues to cry.

As the not-gorillas shuffle farther away,
the child stops crying.

She gets to her feet and dashes
toward the departing group.

The silver-haired male with the tusk
whirls and barks something at her.
The child seizes and goes still,
staring back at him,
slack-jawed and mute.

She steps toward the silver-haired not-gorilla.
He hurls the tusk at her.
Though it goes wide, the child's face
breaks into a frenzied, panicked scream,
and she scampers back to the fallen pair,
throwing her body over them,
face red from crying, red from their blood.

The child stands in the tall grass,
fists balled as she stares after her departing kind.

She kneels in the grass,
shaking the bodies,

so much water running down her face
that it drips off her chin.

The tips of the grass turn orange
as the day's aging sun descends.

They have stayed too late.

The nighttime jungle is already fearsome.
What new dangers does this grassland have?

Snub imagines mountains rolling over the land,
    flattening wayward gorillas,
or tiny jabbering jackals
    swarming out of the black like locusts,
or lions loping low and silent,
    eyes reflecting moonlight.

The only way to keep danger away
is to have a silverback near.

As the sun goes low over the grassland,
Snub senses how far away Silverback is
and her body starts to jangle.

And yet, she doesn't leave.
The not-gorilla child is splayed out in the grass
so low and so motionless
Snub might have forgotten she was there
if it weren't for her
high-pitched keening.

That child has no Silverback near either.

Breath is not interested in a sobbing not-gorilla child.
He rolls out of Snub's lap,
grabs a tuft of thick yellow grass in each hand,
tugs them hard enough
that his body jerks and dances.
He rasps in pleasure at the game.

Snub eases toward the child.

Thick grasshoppers pop away,
flies batter her face,
dry grass crackles.

Breath is never one to be left out.
He bounds onto Snub's back,
raking her hair.
When Snub whirls,
Breath bounces free,
into the grass,
right beside the not-gorilla child.

Her snuffles stop.

Breath scampers up Snub's back.
Once he's secure on her shoulders
he starts making sounds of

wragh

at the child,
beating his little fists on Snub's head
for extra emphasis.

Snub settles him on her back,
and when she returns
her attention to the child,
the not-gorilla has disappeared.

Snub turns around, hooting in confusion.
The grass bursts into yellow motion,
and the child is leaping at her,
hands outstretched and jaws wide open,
leading with her teeth.

They are small teeth,
but Breath cheeps in fear.
Snub flings her arms over her head
and sees the child standing there,
arms still outstretched,
ferocity cooling.

Snub slowly lowers her own arms,
purses her lips and grunts.
The child is a pitiful creature, made more so up close.

She has an oddly bare face,
nearly hairless from brow ridge
to the top of her broad nose,
only the wispiest of hairs
over the brown skin of her neck,
thickening into fullness over her shoulders.
She was well taken care of,
few scars lining her face.
An animal skin is draped over one shoulder,
covering most of her skinny fine-haired body.
The hide smells rancid,
is covered in previous meals,
in the crushed purples and reds of flowers,
the browns of dried mud,
the blacks of dried blood.
Emerging from the bottom of
the animal skin
are impossibly thin ankles,
encrusted in insect bites.

Snub waits for the child to fall down to all fours,
to make a sound of

$$\textit{wragh}$$

or

$$\textit{mrgh.}$$

But she stays silent on her two legs.

The child slowly lowers her arms
and bows her head.

Snub realizes:
She thinks I will eat her.
She is not running.

She wants to be eaten.

Breath gets down from Snub's back,
toddles to the child,
gives her a solid kick on the leg,
then scampers back to the safety of Snub.

The child bares her teeth,
backing toward the bodies
of the two dead not-gorillas,
drawing the rancid animal skin closer
and lying beside them in the grass.

Snub makes a soft grunt and starts away.
If this lonely child tries to follow her,
Snub will not stop her.

But she does not follow.

Snub has been away from Silverback too long.

The setting sun falls behind a rise in the earth
and darkens the land without warning.

The moon has disappeared tonight, as well.
It is too dangerous to walk the jungle.

Snub feels a large fern at the swampy edge of the jungle
and pushes her way into its fronds.
She displaces some small creature
that rustles away through the leaves.
She lowers her body deeper into the stalks of green,
fibers breaking and crackling underneath her.
Breath snuggles down close,
trying Snub's nipple and then
turning so his backside is against her belly.

Snub uproots a sapling and drapes it over them,
sprinkling handfuls of fern on top for warmth.

Nestled away like this,
an elephant or buffalo foraging at night
can't crush them without hitting the tree first.

But the child alone has no such protection.

Night winds whip through the grass,
setting it sighing and screaming.

Snub snuggles deeper into the soft ferns,
clutching Breath as tightly as she can.

Over the sounds of Breath's sleep
and the whip-whistling wind,
Snub hears other noises in the direction of the child.

Panting struggles,
cries of grief
cries of pain
a scream.

Not a scream of pain,
but of some other feeling.

It is still dark,
and yet Snub has come awake.

Breath is awake, too,
clinging to her in silence.

Rain falls,
a hushed patter on the leaves above
under the croaks of frogs,
under the whooshes of bats.

Whatever sound woke them has now stilled.

Careful to make no noise,
Snub retreats as far as she can
into the sheltering hollow of the tree,
pressing into moist wood.

The night world is only frogs and bats and rain.
Then Snub hears a sniffle, and a shuffle.
The ferns beside her rustle.
Breath makes an outraged

wragh.

Snub, suspecting who has arrived,
stays quiet.

Snub is already awake when daylight comes.
She watches gray steal away black.
It starts by lining the edges of a distant stream,
then the puddles of last night's rainstorm.
Finally light arrives to the things that are not water:
the wet hairs on Snub's feet,
the edges of the trees above,
the magnificent lock of red-brown hair
that curls on Breath's sleeping head.

Sunlight arrives on the body beside her.
The not-gorilla child is curled on her side,
knees pressed tight to her chest,
hugging herself.
The soaked animal skin does little to keep her warm.
The droplets on the child's hair tremble with each shiver.

When Snub gets to all fours,
Breath comes with her without even waking up,
snoring away with his fists clutching her hair.
Snub deliberately steps on a branch and cracks it,
hoping the noise will wake the child up.
But she doesn't budge, shut into sleep.

Snub takes a few steps in the direction
of the lagoon, where she last saw Silverback.
After only a few paces,
she finds herself stopping

and looking back at the child holed up in the ferns.
This spindly ape
is so pitiful
and really not so unlike a gorilla.

Snub taps the child's shoulder
with the back of a finger.

The not-gorilla child startles awake,
props herself up on her forearms.

When she sees Snub her eyes widen.
Not just fear—
though fear is there, too.
It is more like she is trying to absorb Snub.

Snub feels *looked at* again.
Breath looks at her this way,
and Mother once did,
but Silverback and Brother do not.

For no reason
the child screams,
a short and piercing noise.

Breath gasps awake,
sees the child,
and gives a sound of

wragh,

angry fingers digging into Snub's skin.

The child—Snub thinks of her as Orphan—
becomes eerily still,
not even raising her hands to defend her face.

Snub makes herself as still as Orphan,
and Orphan stops making noise.
The only movement is Breath
flicking his lips back from his teeth,
which would be scary
if Breath were bigger.
Orphan seems only confused by it.

Snub keeps her eyes trained on Orphan's feet,
not wanting to accidentally present

mrgh.

When she flicks her gaze to Orphan's eyes,
she finds her staring back.
It fires an anger in Snub
for this frail thing to challenge her,
but she remembers Breath doing the same
before he learned how a gorilla should act.

Snub flicks her lips away from her teeth.
That seems to help Orphan understand.
She casts her eyes down to her own feet.

Bobbing her head, Snub turns from Orphan
and roots through nearby nettles
until she comes upon some husks.
The seeds have been eaten,
but there is still plenty of soft white pith
between the inner and outer shells.

Snub pulls out long strands of cottony white fiber.
She places a handful in her mouth.
Breath reaches for his share.

Once she and Breath are both eating,
Snub sneaks a glance at Orphan.
The child watches them, fascinated.

Snub lowers her head, grunts,
holds out the rest of the pith in an
open palm.

Though it is what she hoped for,
Snub is still shocked
when she sees a slender,
soft-haired hand reach in,
work its fingers around the pith,
pull it away.

Orphan gums it down,
going cross-eyed
as she stares along her nose
at the strands falling out of her mouth.

She doesn't know how to eat *pith*.
How can this child possibly survive?

Orphan has finished her handful,
and now looks at Snub hopefully,
a long strand of grubby fiber
dangling from the corner of her mouth.
An ant is on the end,

clutching with its back legs
and raising its head,
antennae tapping.

When Snub reaches forward,
Orphan jerks and goes rigid,
but allows Snub to delicately
take the pith between thumb and forefinger
and raise it to Orphan's lips.

Snub works the fiber into Orphan's mouth
and she swallows it,
ant and all.

Orphan strides away from Snub,
back into the grassland.

The movement is so sudden.
When Orphan swings around a tree and disappears,
Snub is relieved to think that maybe Orphan is leaving,
striking off to find her people again.
Then she's sorrowful,
missing the child who saw her so fully.

Orphan reappears at the far side of the tree,
scrabbling at an open sore in the earth.
She bounds back over,
one of the dirty tubers in hand.
Startled by the sudden movement,
Snub cowers to the earth,
her body shielding Breath.

Orphan waits.

Snub accepts the root and studies its dusty, pitted surface.
She remembers seeing the not-gorillas eat one,
but cannot remember how they started.

Orphan moves so she's in Snub's view,
brings up her hands delicately,
as if there is a tuber in them.
She bites,
pulling at the open space with her teeth.

Snub waits to see what will happen next.

Strange chittery sounds coming from her throat,
Orphan takes the tuber back from Snub.
She places it between her puny canines,
repeats the motion she made before,
this time stripping the bark from the tuber.
Then she passes the clean white flesh back to Snub.

Breath bats at the strange food with his free hand
while Snub brings it to her mouth.

It is watery and crisp.
It is delicious.

Snub would like a tuber to bring back to Silverback and Brother.

Hooting and bobbing,
she approaches the pit where Orphan pulled out the tuber.
But she does not know what to do next.

Orphan is soon beside her, squatting in the soil.
Small rocks and clods fly as she works her way through,
finally getting her fingers under a root.
Snub and Breath grunt in astonishment
as Orphan's veins stand out
while she tries to free it.

She crawls over to the corpses of the not-gorillas,
goes motionless for a moment at the sight of them,
then digs beneath the body of the male until she retrieves
a sharpened stone.

Orphan returns to the pit.
An unknowable not-gorilla expression on her face,
she hacks at the ends of the tuber.
She struggles to lift the large root in both arms,
offers it to Snub.

Snub grasps the tuber in the toes of one foot,
examining its bright glistening flesh.
She decides to take off the bark here,
and her strong teeth make quick work of it.

Once the whole mass of crisp tasty flesh is exposed,
it's hard to resist biting in.

Snub eyes it hungrily.
Breath eyes it hungrily.
Orphan eyes it hungrily.

But Snub tucks the tuber under an armpit
and starts back to Brother and Silverback.

Imagining Silverback's reaction,
Snub goes a long time without thinking about Orphan.

When she remembers her, Snub stops and looks back.
There is no Orphan.

Then Snub sees her, worried,
poking her head around a tree.
Orphan is both hiding and following.

Silverback's nest is still there,
flattened leaves and dry dung,
but he is not.

Knuckleprints surround his nest.

Snub drops the tuber,
then stands on all fours,
sniffing the air for Silverback's scent.

Breath ambles about the clearing,
pretending to investigate trunks and bushes,
but Snub knows his true target.
The tuber.

The wet white flesh has gotten covered
in leaves and dirt and gorilla hair.
Breath bends down near one end,
takes it in his hands,
starts to gnaw.

Orphan approaches,
flitting from trunk to trunk,
half gorilla and half heron.

She heads for the waterfall.
Orphan cranes her skinny body,
trying to get the best view
of the cascade.

Silverback arrives.

He makes his slow and heavy way through the wood,
meaty fists and feet drumming the earth.

When he sights Orphan he gives off a burst of fear-scent.
He opens his mouth to make a sound of

wragh,

but he stops when he sees how near Snub is to Orphan,
how unafraid Snub is.

Orphan turns from her search of the waterfall,
shrieks her strange not-gorilla shriek
at the sight of Silverback,
and cowers behind Snub.

It is the first time they have touched,
and the surprise contact fills Snub with

acha.

Orphan's shriek does something inside Silverback,
setting him racing through the clearing.

Silverback takes a fistful of leaves,
pretends to eat them
so he can expose long teeth
as he stuffs leaves in,
only to let them fall to the ground.
He rises up on his legs and thunders back down.
The ground trembles with the sudden weight of him.
Though there is tension in Silverback's eyes,
he has not hurled anything at Orphan.

Brother bursts into view,
the force of his charge sending him
careening into the ground,
plowing his chin through the dirt.
Then he's back up,
hurtling to Snub and Breath and Orphan.
He rips up an armful of branches,
casts them at Orphan's back.
She hunches even lower,
making herself as small as possible,
her trembling body
never breaking contact with Snub.

Snub whirls to face Brother,
to show him calmness
so he will feel calmness.

Brother brings his lips to Orphan's ear,
mouth open,
breathing on her.
Snub watches Orphan
try to hold still,
face turning red,
lips turning gray.

Then Orphan screams.

Brother kicks at Orphan,
flinging her into the brush.
The not-gorilla child's cry
cuts off.

She emerges sobbing,
hands shielding her face.
But she does not flee.
She huddles under a bush,
curling up as small as possible.

Again Brother charges her.
Snub tries to block him,
but he strikes Orphan with one fist
and then the other.
Each blow empties Orphan's lungs
and creaks her ribs.

Brother's next punch hits her hard
on the back of the neck.
Orphan coughs and goes flat on the earth.

Some day
in the before,
Silverback fought the one
who used to be Silverback.

Another version of this
dragging,
thumping,
screaming.

Unlike a gorilla's tough skin,
Orphan's casing easily splits and parts.
She is soon scored by blood and scratches.

Orphan has stopped crying out,
and as Brother continues to drag her back and forth
she loses the strength to keep her body curled away.

It is not just elbows and knees
raking across the rocky soil.

Silverback holds still, watching and waiting.
Snub has never seen Brother act this way.

Breath squeals in fear
and Brother rushes Orphan,
thumps her again,
grabs her by a heel
and drags her through the brush.

Snub tries to pull her away,
but Brother is too fast,
bringing Orphan bumping over the earth
before Snub can grasp him tightly enough.

Snub watches the whites of Orphan's
panicked eyes
as she's dashed along the ground,
delicate fingers trying to find purchase
but only finding
leaf,
soil,
rock.
Nothing slows her.

Snub has no hope of overpowering Brother,
and she has Breath to worry about.
She can only watch as Brother
stops dragging Orphan,
jumps on her instead,
leading with his heels,
rolling off,
charging back and forth with a branch,
coming to pound her body again.

Orphan doesn't move anymore.
The only sounds from her are
coughs and gasps
whenever Brother's assault
forces the air from her lungs.

Orphan's animal covering has come free during the attack.
Snub can see more of her malformed body,
the places where hair should be but is not,
the odd tilt of her hips,
the long legs,
the frail and nimble hands.

Snub holds one of those hands in hers,
trying this new way
to tell Brother
that Orphan is not an enemy.

At the sight of it
Brother lumbers away
to Silverback.
Silverback's mouth continues to make yawn-threats,
chewing as if there is food between his jaws.

Snub places her whole body over Orphan's.
She and Breath might receive blows,
but putting herself in Brother's way
might be the only way
to prevent the end of Orphan.

Breath wriggles free,
prods Orphan's feet.

Unmoved by Orphan's distress,
he holds on to his own feet
and begins to roll,
rasping at the game
as he careens through the uprooted foliage.

Snub's breathing quickens
when she hears breaking branches;
Brother is on the move again.

As she senses Brother near,
Snub buries her head over Orphan,
chin fitting over the slender nape
of the child's neck.

Snub hears Brother's labored breathing,
Orphan's pained gasps.
Snub waits for Brother's blows to fall on Orphan—
or, worse, on Breath.

But with a grunt of

amrcha,

the shadow of Brother goes away.

Breath's delicate toes rest against Orphan's forehead.
He brings his face right in front of hers,
raps on her temple.

His confusion is clear:
Why isn't she moving?

Snub rolls off Orphan,
sitting on her haunches
to better look at her.

No longer than a gorilla's thumb,
a frog is on Orphan's thigh.
It leaps away into the green.
Snub can't see it amid the leaves,
and realizes the world has gone dim.
Night is almost here.
She has been guarding Orphan
for a long time.

Breath is on Snub's back,
using her body as a nest
since Snub hasn't made them
a proper one.
He snores into her neck.

Orphan is asleep, too.
Sleep is unlike death
because Orphan's back rises and falls,
her mouth agape and drooling.

Snub examines Orphan as best she can
in the scarce light of the evening,
parting the soft hair and grooming
skin gone the color of dead leaves.

She gingerly rolls Orphan over,
sees that the front of her body
has the worst of her wounds.

They've clotted with debris,
dirt and leaves now part of Orphan.

Orphan is shivering in the heat.
Snub picks up the ripped branches
Brother left littering the clearing
and lays them over Orphan's body.

The motion of it wakes Breath.
He squeaks in interest,
promptly goes about undoing her work,
strewing the branches
back around the clearing.

Snub plucks him up,
plants him on her belly.
He whines in protest, but
holds on, making sounds of

acha

as Snub brings the branches back,
tucking them in close to Orphan.

Stirred by the activity,
fat bees crowd the clearing,
their buzz a horror in the nighttime.

Snub tucks herself even tighter around the child,
listening to the sounds of Orphan's breathing,
the echoes of her slow heartbeat under Breath's fast one.

Satisfied that Orphan will live,
Snub allows her eyes to close.

From somewhere far off,
Snub hears a *pap pap.*

It is Silverback, calling her to bed near him.

Snub opens her eyes,
heart surging.

Every habit she has,
every call to maintain

hoo,

the part of her
that longed for home,
for the place that had Mother
and Wrinkled and Teased,
tells her to seek him out.

But instead she waits,
panting at the prickly tension.

Snub imagines Silverback
watching for Snub to come to him,
confused why she has not.

For the first time in Snub's life,
she has not obeyed the call of Silverback.

PART FOUR

NEW MEETS OLD

Snub opens her eyes to see the magpies
poking through a pile of leaves,
lifting each one delicately by its stem,
holding it in the air for a moment's inspection
before casting it to one side.

Their mysterious eyes peer at her,
always from a tilted head,
as if sideways were the best way to see the world.

Orphan breathes slowly and shallowly,
eyes darting beneath purple lids.
During the night Breath switched
from clutching Snub to clutching Orphan,
hands draped across Orphan's slender neck,
snoring into the chill morning.

Snub nudges Orphan,
listens to her nose and mouth.
Orphan continues to breathe.
Her pulse continues to pitter.

Snub grunts and rocks back on her heels.
She moves away from Orphan
and makes a *pap pap* on her chest.
Orphan does not stir.

Snub turns a loose and lazy circle
to make herself dizzy.
She hasn't done this since she was a small gorilla.
She doesn't know why she's doing it now.

Breath climbs up Snub's body to ride her back,
beats an excited rhythm on her shoulders.

Snub will not go far to forage today.
As she and Breath pick through the green,
searching for anything to keep their bellies full,
Snub sometimes goes still and listens,
chin in the air,
hoping to hear the sound of Silverback and Brother,
hoping not to hear the sound of Silverback and Brother.

There is only the hush of the waterfall,
the wind in the leaves,
the calls of birds,
the occasional streak of the magpies overhead.

They remind Snub of something,
of somewhere she once wanted to be.

Young ferns are soft and fuzzy under a gorilla's jaws.
This afternoon Snub has the rare pleasure of a full belly.

She lazes back, holding out a slim green tendril.
She will think about the magpies so she does not
have to think about Silverback and Brother.

The magpie with the wounded leg
hops toward the fern, then stops,
tilting its head quizzically
before hopping forward again.
It nips the stem with its beak.
In her excitement Snub drops the fern,
scrambles to pick it up.

The magpies scatter into the air,
then the wounded one returns
and darts forward again.
This time it seizes the tender stalk,
flaps off to the far side of the clearing.

The other magpie watches its partner
approach Snub and accept another fern.

Breath decides he'll try feeding them, too,
only his idea of feeding a magpie
is to uproot an entire bush
and run at the bird while waving it,
roots raining dirt.

The magpies flee, cawing furiously,
and don't return until near dark,
when they roost in a nearby tree
and look at the gorillas accusingly.

Snub never thought magpies could
glare
but these ones do just that.

Frustrated, Breath stares up into the canopy,
waiting for the birds to come down and play.

Orphan doesn't move for an entire day.

Snub runs the sweetest, most delicate fern head
over Orphan's cracked lips,
over the strokes of dried blood,
but Orphan makes no move to eat.
Her body is as warm as that of an alive creature,
but Snub fears that during the night
it might cool and never warm again.

As before,
she and Breath curl around Orphan's body.
This time Breath doesn't tease Orphan.
He settles in on her back,
reaching his arms wide,
as though shielding her.

As though he is a silverback.

The sun arrives and leaves again
without Orphan moving.

The wounded magpie takes food from Snub's hand again
without Orphan moving.

Breath wanders in and out of the clearing again
without Orphan moving.

Snub feels a tense sort of

hoo

to spend a second day in the same spot,
with the same companions,
all because Orphan can't move.

It is the same sort of peacefulness
as being sick.

Snub is feeding both magpies out of her palm,
Breath sitting on top of her head,
watching with fascination.

Orphan stirs.

She lifts herself to her elbows,
and the birds scatter.

Orphan smacks her hands over her eyes,
gives a howl of pain,
rocks herself.

Breath seems to have forgotten Orphan could be alive.
He hollers at the sight of her,
hides himself away in Snub's lap,
teeth bared even as he faces them the wrong way.
Their sharp points poke Snub's belly.

After her moaning is spent,
Orphan gets to all fours.
She quivers there.
Something wrenches in her back,
and with a gasp of pain
she suffers her way up to two legs.

Orphan taps her spindly fingers against her lips
while looking at Snub.
It is like she is trying to communicate something,
but Snub has no idea what it could be.

Orphan takes a step.

She is back on the ground,
rolling and howling.

Breath,
made miserable by Orphan's misery,
pounds the ground
and kicks out.

Orphan looks at him in shock.
It is the expression a gorilla might make,
jaw slack and brows raised.

She staggers out of the clearing
toward the lagoon,
leaning against the trunks of trees
so that she can keep one leg
from touching the ground.

Snub has avoided the lagoon.
Without Silverback beside them
the sameness of deep jungle feels safer
than being exposed under open sky.

But Orphan heads right there.
She staggers the last few paces to the edge
and kneels beside the water.

What is Orphan doing?

She leans far over,
kissing its surface.

The surf from the waterfall causes the water
to lap over her face,
making her cough even as she sucks water in noisily.

Snub has never thought of eating water.

She looks appraisingly at the surface.
Maybe Orphan knows something she doesn't.
Then Snub shakes her head in disgust.
She will never eat water.

Orphan then does something Snub
has seen only frogs and monitors do:

Orphan jumps into the water!

Snub hoots in fear,
but as soon as Orphan has dropped below
she is back up,
head and shoulders above the surface,
the filth that dried on her body
now floating around her.

Orphan disappears back under,
and is gone for longer this time.

She comes up with a clam.
Snub has seen them before,
these strange rocklike things
that blow bubbles under the water,
but she's never thought to pull one free.

Orphan drops it at the lagoon's edge,
then disappears back under,
returning with a second clam.

She continues until she has a small mound,
then drags herself back to land.

Breath, curious about this new Orphan,
stares into the lagoon.
He splashes at Orphan.
Snub pulls him close to her,
in case he tries to jump in.

Orphan reclines in a patch of sunlight
at the lagoon's shore, eyes closed.

Breath fights to get down.
He nudges and prods the clams,
sending two clattering back into the water.

Once she's dried off,
Orphan presses her body against Snub's
and rubs for a while,
then unsuckers a flat rock from the mud.
She props a clam on the ground, edge up,
and brings the rock smashing down on it.

The two halves fragment and part.
Snub and Breath peer eagerly
and see something that looks
like the inside of an ear.

Is this strangeness inside every clam?
Breath pokes the gooey thing with a toe.

Then Orphan slurps it down!
The thing that looks like an ear!

Orphan forces another open the same way
and hands it to Snub.

Snub looks at it, waiting for the clam to do something.

Orphan takes the clamshell to her lips,
again eats the ear inside.

Snub holds the next one to her mouth.
Breath puts his own face right up to it
as Snub works to eat the clam,
her teeth gnashing the shell.

The slick nugget inside is tough and sweet,
like the glossy bulbs of wild scallions,
though they are both richer and paler.

Orphan offers the next clam ear to Breath,
but he will not have it.
Breath knocks the open shell to the ground.
Orphan picks it up and eats,
displaying her teeth to Snub in a way
that Snub is coming to learn means

                                                acha

when Orphan does it,
not fear.

Time disappears into

hoo.

Sometimes Snub will
smell the scent
of Silverback
and know that
he has slept here.

acha

and fear.

There come many days of rain,
when Snub, Breath, and Orphan huddle under fronds
the shape of large tongues.

One day Orphan ties the fronds
so that they become one thing
that traps more water than before.

From then on,
Snub looks at her like Orphan
is something bigger than Orphan.

Breath is becoming more than Breath, too.
He stops riding Snub,
only holding his arms up to be held
for comfort
when he scents Silverback nearby.

Snub realizes how much Breath
has grown when she looks
for the white tuft on his rear,
the one that makes him easy for
a mother or a sister to spot
even in the dimmest jungle,
and finds that it is gone.

Where are Silverback and Brother?

Snub wonders if they are avoiding her,
which also means
avoiding the furious question of Orphan.

The constant rain is a cocoon,
draws a tight boundary around the day,
washes dirt away from soft roots
and fragrant mushrooms.

The constant rain makes for
wet dawns,
wet twilights,
wet afternoons
spent watching Orphan
crack open clams
at the bank of the lagoon.

While it is raining,
Orphan is in the family.

Whenever the rains ease off
she stares into the distance,
inside herself, like Snub is
when she thinks of Mother.

It gives Snub a flash of

amrcha

to think that Orphan
might prefer to be
somewhere else.

Orphan has a game for Breath
that only Orphan can play:
she holds on to his wrist and an ankle,
then twirls him
so that he is flying through the air,
hair streaming away from wide eyes
and open mouth.

As soon as he's back down on the ground
Breath is back to Orphan,
lifting his arms,
begging to be lifted
and twirled
and made to feel like a bird again.

One night Snub dreams she
is screaming and running.

Silverback charges at her,
only now he wears the white-silver hair
of the not-gorilla
that killed Orphan's mother.

Snub runs and runs,
breathless,
until the jungle changes.
She's rolling down the slope
of the suffering mountain,
surrounded by hot red
that could make her pop and vanish
like she never existed.

Snub wakes up to an ordinary sky
and the coolness of night
but finds the sound that woke her is real,
that Orphan is shaking her shoulders,
panic on her face.

Snub's throat is sore from screams.

In the distance are
the war barks of a gorilla—
of a gorilla fighting.
Silverback.

Snub leaves the clearing,
heading toward the sounds.
Breath lopes alongside her,
Orphan cowering behind,
making her chattery sounds.

Fear-odor.

A boulder rises from the jungle.
This is one of Orphan's favorite places.
She has often climbed it
to sit in the sunshine,
as part of the strangeness of Orphan.

Snub's race toward Silverback's scent
brings her barreling up the boulder

to get a view of below.

Rimmed in the dawn light,
Silverback and Brother are
facing down a group of not-gorillas.

The not-gorillas wield elephant bones,
thumping on the rocky ground,
sometimes sending splinters
flipping into the air.

It makes a terrific noise,
setting Silverback and Brother to cringing
even as they bare their teeth in

wragh.

One of the not-gorillas hurls its bone
in its excitement,
sending it clattering over the stones.

Silverback charges.

He veers to one side before striking the not-gorilla.
The charge opens up his flank,
and one of the creatures casts a sharpened stone,
parting the flesh between two ribs,
setting Silverback roaring
and running back to Brother.
Silverback and Brother were the enemy to Orphan
but they are family when Snub sees
them in danger like this.
She sets her teeth, hair bristling with
feelings of

mrgh.

With not-gorillas blocking the jungle,
Silverback leads a retreat to the only place he can.
To the grassland.

Orphan scrambles forward to yank at Snub's hair
before cowering back into cover.
We need to flee.

The not-gorillas spread out,
yelling unknowable things to one another
as they bloom across the grass.
Brother and Silverback
threat-yawn and make cries of

wragh

as they retreat into the grassland.

Orphan yanks on Snub's arm and points.
Snub can see that the grass has bent,
empty in places.
The earth has bald patches.
Then Snub sees an arm in the air,
signaling.
Each of those empty spots is a not-gorilla,
hidden in the grass
to ambush.
The not-gorillas are hunting
like the wild dogs do.

Snub presses Breath into Orphan's hands.
Startled, Breath bites Orphan's arm,
hops down to the rock.
He glares at Snub in outrage.

Kneeling, Snub picks up a large rock
and hurls it into the midst of the not-gorillas,
hoping only to make noise.

The rock hits the side of the boulder and bounces,
striking out sideways,
striking one of the not-gorillas,
a young female,
on the temple.
She falls where she stands,
now a thing instead of a not-gorilla.

The not-gorillas cry out,
some of them circling the fallen female,
others—including the silver-haired male—
spreading out, looking up.

Seeing Snub and Breath and Orphan.

Fear chases all plans from Snub's mind.
She becomes a creature of reactions,
scrambling over the sunbaked surface
of the boulder
to tumble into the jungle.

Orphan is already moving,
has been waiting for Snub to do just this.
Her hand grips Snub's neck as she guides them
along elephant paths
toward the areas they know,
where not-gorillas
do not go.

Orphan has Breath's hand,
is drag-pulling him along,
even though it gives him
a toddling, awkward gait,
half falling with each step.

Orphan leads through a zagging canyon of crossing trees,
letting go of Snub and Breath
to hold one trunk and swing around and grab the next,
slowing at the end to listen for their pursuers.

Snub's ears fill with tumult:
shouts from the not-gorillas,
crashing branches,
screams of riled monkeys,

screams of riled parrots.
She hopes to hear a sound from
Brother and Silverback,
to know that they are alive,
but she hears nothing from them.

Grabbing a vine that turns into a snake
brings Snub crashing.
She's suddenly looking up at the sky
as the snake skitters into the brush.
While Snub tries to get air back into her lungs,
she sees the two black lines of the magpies,
fleeing
like Snub and Breath and Orphan are
fleeing.

The lagoon.

Orphan skids to a stop
right at the edge,
sending a spray of dirt
plinking into the water.

The distant voice of a not-gorilla.
Orphan springs back into motion,
making panicked moans,
speeding into the green.
Snub tumbles after Orphan,
Breath scrambling between them.

They are fleeing in a direction
where the ground is rocky and
where there are no good plants to eat.
It is the direction where once
was the only blue sky
when all the rest was gray.

It is the direction,
Snub remembers now,
of home.

The jungle gutters out
in a stony plateau.

The rocks, a ferocious orange color
when they were first formed
by the suffering mountain,
have calmed to the grays and browns
of ordinary stone, edges softer than before.
Moss and lichen grow on the roughed ground.
Scrabbly weeds poke through cracks.

With a fearful look over her shoulder,
Orphan starts them onto the plateau.

Never one to be left behind,
Breath toddles after on all fours.

Snub snorts to stop them both.
Hooting with worry, she pivots,
looking now toward the plateau,
now toward the jungle,
with its noises of pursuing not-gorillas.
A fern at the edge of the jungle shakes,
then a not-gorilla tentatively steps out.
It is a young one,
a boy the size of Orphan.

When Snub makes a quiet

wragh

to warn him,
the boy jibbers and shrieks.

Silverback would have charged him.
Snub is not a good silverback.

The boy keeps his jabbering attention on Orphan.

More not-gorillas arrive.
The silver-haired one is in the front.
He makes a gesture with his fingers,
as nimbly as Orphan might have done.

The not-gorillas spread out,
always on their two legs.

Some bang their fists on the rocky ground,
like a gorilla would.
Others grip sharpened stones,
like no gorilla would.

Snub's blood goes solid.
Her pulse flutters at the bottom of her skull.

The not-gorillas are not leery.
They come right near.
Snub's fear stills her,
brings her motionless over Breath and Orphan,
while out of the side of her vision
not-gorilla feet dart
forward and back,
forward and back.

The not-gorillas shout
what Snub has come to recognize
as their version of

mrgh.

Snub screams back in terror,
one arm on Orphan and one on Breath,
whirling,
trying to keep them all safe.

Hands dart in,
hands with something
sharp in them.

Orphan screams,
Breath screams,
Snub screams.

She feels a bright dart of pain on her side,
and she thinks it is from one of their rocks,
but she realizes it is Breath's teeth,
Breath is biting her,
not because Breath is angry
but because Breath is being pulled away
and his mouth is how he holds on.

The not-gorillas are trying to take Breath away.

It is just the mouth and one hand
pulling at her hair now,
Breath's jaw gripping Snub hard enough
that she knows he is drawing blood.
She can feel her muscles pulling
and her flesh tearing, but
is grateful for the pain because it means
Breath is still here.

mrgh.
mrgh.
mrgh.
mrgh.

cowering and biting, snarling and slashing, puny fragile flesh under fingers, little scrap creature hurled against canyon wall, slamming and falling, leg in her mouth and hot salty blood on her tongue, screaming, teeth hitting something hard within muscle, wrenching teeth free, whirling, fingernails and stones on her, Orphan safe to one side, female struggling to keep Breath in her arms, his hysterical eyes on Snub, arms reaching for her, another not-gorilla wrenching Breath's arm, pulling him in two, trying to pull Breath in two, a vision of little arms and legs, too far from the rest of Breath,

mrgh.

hurtling toward not-gorillas, backbones under fingers and toes, small knobby bones crunching under sprays of blood, Breath is back to her, Breath is whole, Breath is in Snub's arms, Orphan cowering on the plateau, sobbing into her knees, no saving both Breath and Orphan, one rescued the other taken, flee, across the plateau and away from green, Breath clamps on to belly, hands and feet free to sprint, no sight of not-gorillas, but sound, horrible sound, a slavering tower at her back, propelling past Orphan, seeing Orphan rise to her feet, Orphan fleetly following

mrgh.

imagining sharp stones slicing into Breath, racing faster and faster, grunting in terror, stopping, Orphan stopping Snub by biting into her leg, Snub realizing she's been dragging the child along, Orphan's spindly body skidding on rocks, Snub releasing Orphan, Snub heaving in air, the plateau is silent.

The not-gorillas have not followed.

Orphan is curled on the ground, crying.
Breath is still clamped tight to Snub's chest.

Snub stands as tall as she can on all fours,
her blinding

mrgh

slowly draining.

Snub can think again.

She nuzzles Orphan,
hoping to provide some comfort and
needing
Orphan's comfort in return.

Orphan shows no feeling on her face now.
Orphan has disappeared into Orphan.

Snub climbs a tall rock to look back.

The not-gorillas have not left.
Neither are they following.
They stand silent where the plateau begins.
Not daring to follow.

The plateau has no food on it.
It has barely any green at all.

Sun beats without mercy.
Its heat gnaws at Snub's thoughts,
scrambling and stealing them.

Salty water appears in Orphan's hair,
beads in the light.
Snub grooms it from her, but more comes.

Snub loses track of their direction,
does not know which way they are meant to go,
so Snub doesn't move her family forward or backward.

They chase the shade
as the sun shifts in the sky.
They hunker down, licking cracked lips
during the hottest center of the day.

They spend a night huddled together on the rocky ground,
in an unknown place, without a silverback.
    Is Silverback alive? Is Brother?
Come dawn, Snub finds it hard to move.
Everything aches.

Orphan is the one to start them along the plateau,
heading away from the sun
and the not-gorillas.

She is nervous to lead,
flipping her lips from her teeth and back,
cringing and looking to Snub for comfort,
sometimes collapsing to the ground, overwhelmed,
waiting for Snub to groom her
before continuing on.

As the heat increases,
Breath is an unmoving weight at Snub's chest.

Though fear of the not-gorillas
keeps Snub's mind tense and overfull,
like a sunned blister,
setting her head to aching,
the not-gorillas have not followed.

As Snub and Orphan and Breath
press forward through the day,
the green begins to return.

Breath is alive, but he is still, still, still.

The canyon opens out
into a meadow
that Snub remembers.

Here they once spent the night in yellow grasses,
Here they followed a gully filled with cormorants
escaping the black ash pond.

Here is closer to home.

Snub leads them to the center of the meadow,
where a dim memory tells her Silverback
once brought them to browse.

Within the thick blades are shoots young enough to eat.
As Snub settles her family in to forage,
she finds herself craving the wetness
inside the grass more than its taste.

As more and more grass goes into Snub's belly,
her headache begins to withdraw.
It has been so much a part of her
she stopped noticing it.

At first Breath will barely open his eyes.
He's left trails of dung all down Snub's body.

Snub takes a big mouthful of grass in,
chews it into a wad,
pries Breath's mouth open with her fingers,
and drops it in.

He blinks at her, surprised,
his eyes opening fully
for the first time all day.

Then he chews and swallows,
wincing as he forces the pellet of food
down his throat.

Orphan stays close.
She watches Snub eat, then
chews on some of the youngest blades.

Orphan looks confused,
as if eating grass is strange, when
it is Orphan who is strange.

The magpies land right next to Snub,
picking through the grass,
looking for a meal in the same place.

Snub does not mind, because magpies
eat things that gorillas will not eat,
spiders and egg sacs and pale wriggly grubs.

One of them uses Breath's foot as a perch.
Snub watches the bird peck at the earth.

The hunt for green to eat
leads Snub's family
steadily toward the dark pond.
Toward what was once home.

Where has the pond gone?

At first Snub thinks she is in a different place,
that she has been mistaken.

Then she realizes that the pond
has been replaced by a new meadow,
by a thick circle of feathery,
powdery greens and powdery browns,
broken by rotting trunks of fallen trees.

The same kind of monkeys that Snub remembers
clinging to the floating tree during her dark night
scamper up and down,
hopping to the lush soil,
then into the fallen tree's branches.

Snub noses into the open area.
Orphan's hand is on one flank,
Breath's hand is on the other.

Wildebeests graze the new grasses at the far side,
but these animals do not put fear in Snub's heart.
She makes her way forward more boldly now
into the place where
land has filled the pond.

Snub stops, heart seizing.

Her body falls into panic,
her throat grunting

wragh.

Her hands beat her chest and
her legs run her in tight circles.

As she hurtles, her mind catches up to what she saw.

A monster cascading down the slope.
A giant slug, longer than any creature should be,
a shiny black thing as long as the mountain is tall.

Frightened by Snub's terror,
Breath dashes behind her,
screaming,
little arms flailing.

They are out of the meadow and deep in the jungle,
huddled at the base of a tree,
before Snub realizes that Orphan is not with them.

Worry for Orphan overcomes worry for herself.
Snub threads through the trees,
she and Breath calling out

wragh,

fear pungent all around them.

Snub prepares for the sight of Orphan
snared in the giant black slug's tendrils.

But she finds a curious sight:
Orphan is not at all afraid.
She is standing right next to the slug
that reaches to the top of the crater.
She is tapping its black flesh.
It rings out.
It is not flesh.

Orphan turns toward Snub, wonder on her face,
and points into the surface of the big black thing.

Snub and Breath cautiously make their way over.
At first the surface is all dancing light,
but then Snub makes out
two black forms on all fours,
one larger and one smaller,
and one lighter-colored figure on two legs.
They are all staring back at Snub.

Seeing foreign gorillas,
Snub fills with a feeling of

wragh,

beats her chest and races
to the far side of the shining black
to better see the gorillas trapped
inside the stilled stone slug.

But the gorillas face her on the other side,
too, only now they're in pieces,
colliding in front of her eyes,
disappearing entirely when Snub charges them.

Why is Orphan not scared?
She makes soothing sounds toward Snub.
She raps her knuckles against the black shiny surface,
making it ring out again.

Calmed by Orphan's calm,
Snub stares into the black stone
while the dream gorillas glint back.

When she is not aggressive toward them,
they are not aggressive toward her.

When she bares her teeth at them,
they bare their teeth at her.

It is up to Snub what those gorillas will feel.
It is like she is a silverback.

Snub now knows this enormous black thing
is no animal but something else,
a part of the land.
This is where the mountain's suffering
once streamed a hot river,
only now it has cooled and hardened
so it is a shiny sort of stone
that reflects like the surface of a puddle.

It traces the whole length of the ruined mountain
up to the top of the fallen crater ridge.
It is a scab of the land's old wound.

If Snub followed this scab up,
she would be back in her old home.

If it is still there.

Snub keeps her distance
as she follows the black scar,
clambering over rocks and soil.

The earth is still ravaged,
but its edges have softened,
are covered with soft green fuzz,
tendrils of struggling plants,
beginnings of bushes and trees.

Snub runs her fingers
along the tops of the greenery,
yanks up handfuls of it,
pressing buds into her mouth.
This soft green is all young,
This soft green can all be eaten.

As they near the top of the crater ridge,
the plane of the mountain's scar expands.
Orphan is the first to step onto the glossy surface,
holding an outcropping with one hand
before placing one foot and then the other
on uneven ground.
The rock frays and crunches under her feet.
She makes a few leery steps,
then puts all her weight down,
bobbing her head toward Snub.
Come.

Breath climbs to Snub's back
as she starts forward.
The shiny surface crunches and splinters
beneath her fingers and toes.
It is like walking across a field
of freshly broken bamboo.
It is not sharp enough to hurt Snub,
but Orphan's skin parts for it,
latticing the soles of her feet with red.

Snub feels a strange inversion of

hoo

to approach this land
that used to be all she knew,
to climb the stone memory
of the mountain's pain,
with her new family of
a young gorilla
a young not-gorilla.

Breath fusses to get down from Snub.
As soon as he's on the sharp terrain
he raises his arms to be lifted back up.
Snub places him across her belly,
like he is a younger gorilla than he is,
and hurries to catch up to Orphan.

The familiar old lake has come back.
The brown-blue of the water
has taken on a new shape,
is now a long and skinny oval overhung
by an enormous new rock.

Around it are surviving trees,
some standing tall but others growing sideways,
upheaved.

The ground is dotted in light greens:
ferns and stonecrop,
the beginnings of larger plants,
all of it edible.

Home.

Overcome, Snub sits right where she is.
Breath wriggles out from under her.

Orphan leads them forward.

The climb down is hard—
it would be difficult for an animal
without feet,
like a rhino or an elephant.
Maybe even the wild dogs
could not get over these rocks.

hoo.

Where are Silverback and Brother?
They are not here.
They have not been with Snub for a long time.
Even still, her heart is baffled to be here,
home, without the rest of her family.

hoo

without them is a different sort of

hoo.

Soon there will be
familiar rocks and trees,
favorite napping spots!
Snub clambers down the rock,
grunting in excitement.
Breath gets down and walks alongside her
once the grass begins,
tumbling and grunting in pleasure.

As they barrel along, Snub realizes that Orphan is not following.

She looks back to find Orphan
sifting through shards of black shiny rock,
testing each one by hefting it in her hand
before shaking her head,
casting it to the ground.

She finally selects one,
gripping it tight as she starts down the slope.

Even though she is family now,
Orphan is still a not-gorilla.
Orphan still wants a sharpened rock.

They will not travel to the very center of home.
Snub does not wish to be reminded
of the worst
of the mountain's suffering.

As Snub leads her family
into the trees,
monkeys scatter.
These are not the small brown ones
that used to live here.
These monkeys have long black hair,
a white stripe down the middle of their backs.

Maybe the mountain spat these monkeys out
after it finished spitting out the hot river.

Once they're deep into the trees,
Snub brings her family to a stop,
stands on all fours,
breathing in the humid air,
full of the scents of leaves,
of mud,
of decay,
of food.

She lets her eyes travel the scene,
like Silverback once would have done.

Snub had thought she would have to find a new home.
But it has been here all the time,
recovering.
Waiting for them to return.
For some of them to return.

The magpies arrive soon after Snub and her family,
arrowing into the upper reaches of a tall palm.
Their home is so high!
When Snub tries to see them
she is dazzled by sunlight,
can make out only their vague shapes
as they dart in and out of the fronds.

Snub and Breath barely go more than a few paces in a day,
picking through the grasses for the choicest seeds and blades.

Orphan wanders farther,
sometimes disappearing for long enough
that the sun is on the other side of the sky
when she returns.
She departs in a corridor flooded with light.
She reappears in a corridor flooded with shadow.
It makes Snub wonder
what happens inside Orphan.

Once Orphan appears at the clearing's edge,
making sounds that Snub now knows
are Orphan's version of

amrcha.

Orphan gets her sharp black stone in hand
before starting back out of the clearing.
She looks over her shoulder,
chattering at Snub.

Snub shakes her head, confused.

Breath heads to Orphan, excited,
tripping through the clearing.

Snub follows more cautiously.
Orphan is leading them into the center of home,
where the mountain's suffering first started,
where the lake fell
where animals burned
where Snub's long journey first began.

Even as Snub grunts in protest,
Orphan urges them onward, faster and faster.

Snub stops and gives a roar like
Silverback might have made.
Snub makes the loudest *pap pap* that she can.

Orphan stops and stares at Snub,
a pleading look on her face.

Their wills tug at each other.
Wind whistles through the trunks,
casting up eddies of willowy insects
and caterpillar-laced leaves.

Then the wind dies.
Beneath it Snub hears what Orphan has heard,
what has made Orphan so urgent.

In the distance
a gorilla is making hooting sounds.
A gorilla is in distress.

When Orphan starts out again,
Snub follows willingly,
Breath tight on her back.

Though Orphan is fleet in the open spaces,
slinking ahead easily on her two legs,
it is Snub who manages better
once the overgrowth closes in,
taking to the trees to cross a ravine
that Orphan must ford.

The gorilla cries are ever louder.

Snub feels

acha,

but she struggles to remember what gorilla this is,
why this voice would make her feel this way.

Snub loses her balance.
Breath makes outraged grunts
as he tumbles free onto all fours.
He rips up a single nettle,
charges Snub with it.
But Snub pretends not to notice.

A gorilla should not travel along a ravine.
Soggy dead plants are at the bottom,
coated in pond muck.
Snub's hands and feet squish into it,

making sounds that fill her with disgust.
Snakes scatter before her,
hiding away in matted reeds.

Snub sneaks by them nervously.
Orphan continues to flit forward
as if she has lived her life in ravines,
as if she has never been afraid of a snake.
Breath lumbers to Orphan,
unaware of a bright green praying mantis
that has climbed onto him.
It clutches his ear for balance.

When Breath reaches Orphan,
he stares where Orphan stares,
mouth open.

As Snub reaches them,
the sounds of the distressed gorilla
broaden and echo,
as if this upset gorilla
were a creature made of rocks.

A cave entrance,
large enough to fit two gorillas shoulder to shoulder.
The sunlight survives only a few lengths into the space
before dying, leaving the rest of the interior dark.

Orphan steps in and then steps out with a shriek,
looking to Snub for comfort.
On all fours, Snub stares hard into the black,
as if staring hard means seeing better.

She risks making a call, briefly getting up on two legs
so she can give her chest a *pap pap* with no

wragh

in it.

Who are you?

The gorilla inside the cave stops its cries.

Snub makes another *pap pap*.

The distant gorilla makes a surprised, strangled noise.
Snub hears scrabbling,
the sound of a rock falling,
something heavy and soft
hitting the ground and tumbling.

She hoots tentatively.
She is hearing a gorilla
that she once knew very well.

There is silence, then the cave gorilla makes a sound of
                                                    acha.

Snub surges into the darkness,
stones clattering away under her hands and feet,
thinking only of heading toward the
                                                    acha

of the gorilla
that she thought she'd never hear again.

The cave's darkness hides its slickness,
and she's slipping.
Breath is on her back,
scrambling and sliding with her.
Snub can hear Orphan tumbling
somewhere behind her,

clattering to the ground
before lurching up,
clattering to the ground again,
sending soft silvery rocks
tinkling into the blackness.

Between grunts and calls of

acha

the cave gorilla makes click sounds,
like she is suckering her tongue
from the roof of her mouth
again and again.
As Snub scrambles forward,
bashing into unseen rocks,
she sees outlines,
enough that she can start to avoid them,
until the cavern becomes light enough
that she can see color,
like the cave up ahead has its own small sun.
The walls around her
are made of the same glossy black stone
that formed the motionless black slug
on the side of the mountain.
Snub realizes that she is now *inside* the mountain.
Silvery flecks deep within the vaulting stone walls
glitter when they catch the light.
Cave roaches skitter, each as big as Snub's foot.
There are bats on the ceiling, too,
volleys of them flapping at Snub's face,
Breath reaching out but failing to catch them.
Snub realizes she has been hooting in fear
only when she switches to sounds of confused

A gorilla that Snub thought
was gone forever
has been returned.
Getting her back makes Snub
feel the rage of losing her
all over again.
At the bottom of the pit of sunlight,
cowering and pale,
surrounded by the pearlescent wings of old roaches,
is Mother.

PART FIVE

HOME REMEMBERED

Mother wags her head vaguely in Snub's direction,
makes a whimper filled with

acha,

staggering to all fours before sitting back down,
holding out her arms
to hold Snub,
to be held by Snub.

How matted Mother's hair is,
how scarred and milky her eyes,
what stink on her skin and in her breath.

Snub clutches Mother tight to her,
feels the sharp bones of Mother's back,
the ribs of her.

There is no feeling
better than this.

A cramp in her leg finally forces Snub to pull away.
She catches sight of the source of the cavern's light,
a hole in the roof where the rock has crumbled.

Light streams through,
motes and flecks of black
suspended
in the column of yellow sunshine.

Above, Snub can see leaves and sky.
Down here are whispery shufflings:
cave roaches and fluttering bats.

Snub can understand why Mother would return home,
even if she can't fathom how.
But why would Mother choose to live down here?

Snub shifts into the column of light
so it fully catches Mother's face.
One eye is gone,
and the other is surrounded by scars,
like a fractured stone.
In the center of the scar web,
where an eye should be,
is something that looks like
a smooth shell instead.

Snub tugs Mother toward the exit.
Maybe in the sunlight
that gray orb will take back its color.
Maybe in the sunlight
Mother will see again.

Mother pulls away and makes
clicking sounds with her tongue,
cocking her head and listening after each one.

Mother makes a click,
pauses,
then clicks again.
Somehow she senses
Orphan and Breath,
hovering and uncertain
at the edge of the light.
Mother takes a step toward them.

Orphan's eyes glimmer with curiosity
as she stares at Mother.

Breath is undone.
He looks at Mother like he is looking at something
that used to be part of his body.
His attention is on her even as his legs
work him backward
into the dark of the cave.

His foot skitters a loose stone
and he squeaks in surprise,
glaring at the ground.

At the sound of his voice,
Mother works her way to him,

moving half like a gorilla,
half like a river crab,
easily keeping clear
of the rocky cavern walls.

Bats volley before her,
buffeting Breath's face,
setting him squealing.
He runs down the cavern,
disappearing into the darkness.

Mother stops where she is,
head cocked to one side.
She clicks her tongue
but doesn't seem to understand
the sounds echoing back to her.

Mother starts toward Breath,
easily navigating the dark cave,
clicking and pausing,
leading Snub between obstacles
that she never sees,
massive bulks passing in the quiet dark.

Snub keeps close to Mother's back.
Orphan keeps close to Snub's back.

Mother halts at the exit.
She makes her clicking sounds
but doesn't seem satisfied
with whatever she gets back.

Snub presses her whole body against Mother,
letting her know that she is beside her.
Mother lets Snub lead her into the sunshine.

Breath startles and runs
farther off,
then stops himself.

For long moments they are all motionless.
Mother's chest is craggy and rough
where the wounds of the not-gorillas'
attack have scarred her.
One of her fingers
and two of her toes

have broken and re-formed
at tilted angles.
The skin Snub can see wherever
Mother's thinning hair parts
is moon white.

Mother is in each of Snub's memories of home,
even the earliest ones.
She was here long before Snub.
Even blinded, her link to this place drew her here,
surviving by fingers and nose and ears,
so great was her will to come back.

Here is home returned,
fragile and soft and small.

Here is Mother returned,
fragile and soft and small.

Step by cautious step,
Breath approaches her,
making sounds of

                                    amrcha

that gradually shift to

                                    acha

as he sees her up close.

He waits for Mother to come pick him up
like she once did.

But Mother is looking the wrong direction,
head swiveling uselessly,

her clicks telling her little about her world.
Her focus trains on Orphan, and Snub wonders:
Without sight, does Mother know what Orphan is?
Does she think Orphan is a gorilla?

Breath lifts a hand to poke Mother in the neck.
She whirls on him, teeth bared.
Breath recoils, cowering,
but he returns his finger to her,
this time laying it
on her frail and balding neck,
as if to hold in the pulse of her veins.

Mother startles again,
then lowers her head.
Breath reaches his other hand to her neck,
peering into Mother's ravaged face.

He tries to climb onto Mother.
She gasps at the strain on her body
and he slips from her.
Mother wraps her arms around
her own rickety frame
and rocks.

Breath cries like he hasn't cried
since he was the pink worm.

Snub grooms him.
While she does, she sees
Orphan hover near Mother.
Mother points her face in Orphan's direction

for only a moment
before training it back on the ground.

Snub makes soft hoots of warning
as Orphan eases closer, then closer.
Trembling, Orphan lays her hand
on Mother's frail shoulder.
Mother sighs.
Mother has not been touched in a long time.

Orphan places another hand on Mother's back,
gentler than Breath.
Mother sighs deeper.
Orphan wraps her long skinny body
around Mother,
holds Mother,
her cheek resting on the crown of Mother's head.

Water forms in the corners of Orphan's eyes
and tumbles into Mother's matted hair.

Snub and Breath hold each other
while they watch
Orphan hold Mother,
doing something no gorilla would do,
comforting a stranger.

Orphan holds Mother
until Mother stops rocking herself,
until Mother falls asleep.

Does Mother know that Orphan is not a gorilla?
Does Mother know that Breath is her son,
now twice as big as when he was last beside her?

Snub cannot know what Mother knows.
but she knows the

hoo

of having Mother and Breath and Orphan with her.

Snub watches Breath
scrambling around the family:
pulling hair,
whacking with sticks,
running off,
grunting with joy,
tenderly tucking in at night
in the midst of them all,
hands and feet on
Snub and Orphan and Mother
so that he is touching
them all at once.

When Mother wakes she gets to all fours,
puts her nose in Orphan's direction,
face wagging until Orphan gets up.

Mother is bad at grooming herself.
She will leave the husk of a dead worm
smooshed into her back,
attracting a stream of ants.
It is up to Orphan to groom it out,
delicately unsticking the corpse.

It confuses Snub
that Orphan could come from the not-gorillas,
beasts violent as crocodiles,
yet show such

                                                        acha

to Mother.

Breath wanders farther each day,
but it is never hard to find him.

He can't go too long without making noise,
shrieking with excitement
when he comes across a fallen junglesop fruit,
or causing a ruckus of breaking branches
when he chases an antelope baby into its den.

Sometimes he's quiet, letting Mother take
one of his little feet in her hand,
holding it to her face like
a flower she's afraid to crumple.

The magpie with the curled leg
is making a fuss on its branch,
hopping around
and pecking at something out of view.

The other magpie soars out and soon returns,
a blade of grass in its mouth.
The magpie with the curled leg seizes it,
while its mate zooms off to pick another.

Backgrounded by the clear blue skies,
swaying green trees,
life is as it once was and always will be.

The magpies are building a nest.

Orphan is eating a piglet.

Snub does not know where she found it,
but Orphan is splitting its corpse like a ripe fruit,
digging dirt-crusted thumbnails into the
piglet's torso and parting it.

The rib cage splits,
exposing red and purple and gray inside.
Orphan runs each organ beneath her nostrils,
like buds.

She offers every morsel to Snub first,
held out in gory fingers.
Each time Snub turns her head away and grunts.

Orphan smacks the piglet down happily,
eventually giving up on Snub,
offering bits to Mother instead.

Mother is even less interested,
snorting and turning her head away
each time Orphan brings a bloody bit to her nose.

Finally Orphan gives up on them both,
cracking the small bones,
sucking the insides of each one
before throwing it in the grass.
Like that, there is no more piglet.

Soon there will be no memory of piglet
either.

The rummaging magpie with the curled leg
notices the bones.

It flits down to land right on Mother.
She raises her hands,
as if stroking the air surrounding the bird.
The magpie hops along Mother's belly,
slender black legs stark against the gorilla's pale skin.

The magpie flits to the grass,
pecks up a shard of
one of the piglet's
delicate rib bones,
soars up to the treetop.
Its mate examines the bone
before accepting it,
retreating into the greenery.

The magpie with the curled leg
is soon on the ground again,
picking out another bone,
flying it back up.

It is after dawn,
and Orphan is crouching nearby.
This morning the not-gorilla child has no eyes
for Breath or Mother or the magpies.
Only for Snub.

Orphan gives Snub a long look,
then soundlessly heads out of the clearing.

Snub doesn't want to leave Breath and Mother behind,
but she cannot refuse Orphan's urgent expression.

As Snub follows Orphan,
one last look back tells her that Mother
isn't even aware that they've left.
She is serenely feeling her way through the grasses,
taking nibbling samples before deciding
whether to commit to eating the whole thing.
Breath lies on his back with his eyes closed,
content to be with Mother.

Orphan goes fast, and Snub is glad.
She does not want to leave Mother and Breath
alone for long.

When they reach the tinkly-crunchy scree
near the crater's rim,
Orphan drops to all fours and begins to slink.

As she picks her way over the sharp rocks,
Snub hears a chaos of sounds from below,
speeds up to see what it is.

Orphan tugs at Snub's hair,
points down the slope
toward Breath and Mother.
Snub bats her hand away.
What is Orphan so worried about?

Orphan yanks roughly on Snub's hair.
Snub bats her away harder,
sending Orphan sprawling into the scree,
bits of sharp glossy stone
cascading into the meadow and forest
at the far side.

Snub is fascinated by the rockslide,
watches the glittering black flecks
tumble into the forest line.

That's when she sees it.
The trees are moving.

Gorillas are racing up the crater slope,
toward Snub and Orphan's hiding spot.

At the front are two silverbacks.
One is large and muscular.
The other is not silver-powerful but silver-old.
He moves with stiff, pained movements,
sometimes splaying into the rocks,
only picking himself up with effort.

They're followed by three more gorillas.
All rush up the slope,
looking back over their shoulders as they go.
They are fleeing something.

More figures appear behind them,
almost like gorillas
but on two feet,
animal skins tied around their bodies.
They brandish rocks and bones.
They gibber and holler.

More and more arrive,
silhouetted by the misty sun.

They move slowly as they trail the gorillas.

The not-gorillas are hunting gorillas again.
The not-gorillas have come to Snub's home.
The not-gorillas are invading Snub's home.

From back within the jungle,
Breath makes a sound of

wragh.

The small sound soon disappears.

Snub cries her own

wragh

and races toward Breath and Mother.

Orphan is right beside her, making the furious
noises of a gorilla
and sometimes
the furious noises
of a not-gorilla.

Once they're within the hush of the canopy,
where there has been such

hoo,

Snub calms some.

Orphan doesn't slow for a moment.
She scrambles on through the brush,
jabbering as she whips through ferns and vines.

Mother and Breath have heard their noisy approach.
Mother is up on all fours.
Breath catches Orphan's fear and
*pap pap*s his chest once,
twice.

It is more a soft pop than a proper thud.
He is young yet.

Snub places a hand on Breath's backside,
where once there was the tuft of an infant.
Breath climbs onto her back.

Snub turns,
steps this way and that,
unable to think of how to keep
Snub and Orphan and Mother and Breath
alive if the not-gorillas charge into their home
with their sharpened rocks.

Orphan grooms Mother ruthlessly,
though she is not looking at Mother
but in the direction of the not-gorillas,
accidentally pulling out a clump of Mother's hair
even as she makes sounds of

                                                    acha.

Mother whines.

Palm trees part with a ferocious crack.
The first of the gorillas careens through,
speeding into the clearing,
intent on the far side.

The older, grayer silverback runs right up
to the huddled mass of Snub and her family,
almost knocking them over before
he sees them and hurls his body to one side,
skidding through muck and debris.

He rears in alarm,
teeth bared in the

mrgh

that is surprise.

He beats his chest,
preparing to charge.

He stops.

Snub disentangles from the
cowering bodies of Orphan and Mother.
She steps to one side,
head bowed submissively
but not so much that she cannot
continue to watch.

If it weren't for the shape of his nose,
Snub might not have recognized him.
He has changed so much.
Silverback's face is still broad and sturdy,
but the hair on it is patchy,
leaving stretches of skin bare,
exposing a long scar on the chin.
His lower lip sags on one side,
as if that spot is not part of Silverback,
as if he has decorated himself
with the lip of another gorilla.
His expression is no longer one of

wragh.

It is one of fear.

Silverback copies Snub's submissive position,
forehead bent toward the muddy ground.
Snub is confused.
Silverback does not act like a silverback anymore.

When she hears Silverback's voice
and smells his pungent fear-scent,

Mother is up and alert,
facing his general direction,
wagging her face in the air.

Orphan scrambles to her feet.
That's when Brother arrives.

He enters at a stately pace,
pushing aside the fronds of a fern
before stepping into the clearing.
He's half again larger than the last time Snub saw him,
his flat back bulked and broad.
Brother's head, which used to seem too large,
now triangles into the muscles of his shoulders.

Brother sees Snub, and it stills him.
Brother sees Mother, and it softens him.
Brother sees Orphan, and it enrages him.

He goes rigid, the muscles along his arms and legs cording.
He makes first one step toward Orphan and then another,
now running,
now teeth bared,
now beating his chest.

Orphan screeches, hair flying
as she dashes to the nearest tree.
Snub rushes to Orphan's aid,
but Brother whirls on her,
swiping her to the ground.
Snub hits heavily,

wind knocked out of her,
vision sparking.

Brother beats on the tree.
Orphan is well up by now,
gripping a branch,
peering down.

Mother makes a shriek of protest,
surprisingly loud from such a rickety creature.
Brother listens.
Silverback listens.
All the gorillas in the clearing still.

Snub sees that Mother's focus is not on Orphan,
but on the distant crater rim,
invisible through the dense jungle.
Mother's hearing is better than
any of theirs.

Silverback, too, becomes distracted
by the crashing sounds there,
by the jabbering cries of the not-gorillas.

He begins to ease toward the far side of the clearing
even as his gaze remains focused on
Brother, pounding Orphan's tree.

More noises come through the jungle,
drawing even Brother's attention.

The new female gorillas have arrived.
Unlike the silverbacks these three are shy,
pulling up vegetation
as soon as they are in view,
making great shows of eating it
to put the strangers at ease.
To put Snub at ease.

She finds herself making similar movements,
sneaking glances at the strangers
through the sides of her eyes
as leaves fill her view.

It is something Snub has wanted
for such a long time,
new gorillas to be with.
These three are young,
not young like Breath
but young like Snub,
females with soft eyes,
curiosity within their fear.
Part of her wants to groom them,
part of her wants to ignore them entirely
and only
flee,
flee,
flee.

The not-gorillas are making
their jibbering calls,
coming ever nearer.

Old Silverback is the first to bolt.
The sweet-eyed female gorillas stop pretending to eat,
move to follow him,
but then hesitate when they see that Brother is not leaving
the tree where Orphan is hiding.
The young silverback looks
toward the sounds of the not-gorillas,
then makes a

wragh,

directed neither at them nor at Orphan
but at some space in between.

Brother tosses his head haughtily,
races after Silverback,
out of the clearing.

The female gorillas stream after him.
The last one takes
a wistful look
back at Snub
before she disappears.

Snub rushes to Orphan's tree,
taps her hands on the trunk.
We need to go.

Orphan lowers herself down,
branch by branch,
until again she is with Snub.

Breath is full of vigor without direction,
staring after Silverback and Brother
and the new gorillas,
then whirling,
his attention on the crater ridge and
the sound of the not-gorillas.

It has started to rain.
Here beside Snub is a growing puddle,
there above, raindrops patter the leaves.

The magpie with the curled leg
soars up to its nest,
shaking water from its feathers
before disappearing within.

Mother totters her way along the wet jungle floor,
pausing to click at every step,
making her way toward the sound of Snub's

acha,

toward Orphan's labored breathing,
toward Breath's confused hoots.
She huddles in with her family
as the air turns misty, soaking them all.

There is a noise from within the jungle,
the unmistakable jabber of a not-gorilla.
Then all goes silent.

Maybe the not-gorillas will never approach.

The magpies make their clucks and caws
before then they, too, settle into their nest.

The rain has brought back the possibility of

hoo.

Snub wants to be with the other gorillas,
but Mother could never move fast enough to catch them.
Breath couldn't either, unless Snub carried him,
and she would soon tire.
Worst of all, Brother might kill Orphan.

To journey with Silverback and Brother,
Snub would have to abandon
her family
and her home.

She will never do that,
so they will all have to stay here,
in the homeland that once was lost.

Because she doesn't know where to go,
Snub rests.
She is hidden as best she can be
in the hollow of a tree
with her family.

She strokes the reddish curl on Breath's head,
runs her hands along his shoulders and arms.

Orphan joins Breath on Snub's lap,
her legs sprawled in the mud
but her head and shoulders
on Snub's thigh.
Snub comforts her, too,
and then grooms through Mother's sparse hair.
Somehow in the midst of all this
Mother has fallen asleep.
Her breathing is shallow but regular.

Awake but growing sleepy,
Snub stares up at the magpie nest.
Every once in a while,
one of the birds will step
out onto the branch,
hop to the tip,
see if it is still raining,
then hop back toward shelter.

Distantly, Snub hears the excited call of not-gorillas.
Snub imagines that they have found an animal
and made it into a carcass.

Maybe the not-gorillas will never voyage deep enough
into the jungle to come upon this clearing.
Maybe Snub and her new family will be able to live here forever,
find

hoo

that will last forever.

In this dream
Snub is small,
small like Breath.
Mother is as Snub
once knew her,
healthy and strong.

Together
they wander a land
without sharpened stones,
a land
of quiet green,
of quiet black,
a broad belt of gorilla jungle.

Snub's body is thrashing before she wakes up.
Her limbs surge and batter,
claw out at the bright intensity
in her neck
that she's realizing is pain.

She's pummeling a not-gorilla;
a not-gorilla has ambushed her in the dim light of dawn,
has brought one of its sharpened rocks
down on Snub's throat
to get her to release her blood
and suffer
like the mountain
once suffered.

Heat soaks Snub's chest
as she punches
the cowering creature,
as she feels its limbs break,
its skull smash.

Only after the not-gorilla has become a corpse
does Snub see it's a young not-gorilla,
a boy no larger than Orphan.

There is so much blood,
it makes Snub's fingers slip.

The world is roaring
filled with white
weightless
painless
Snub-less.

She is lighter than being.
She is

                                        hoo,
                                       acha,
                                     amrcha,

she is the love she has for Breath and Orphan and Mother,
mouths wide open and fists flailing the ground.
They are upset,
upset
about what is happening to Snub,
but Snub is the blossoming white of the world
that fills her eyes
lifts her limbs
joins ground with face
only *it's* not ground at all
but strangely sky.

Orphan is dragging the not-gorilla carcass
out of the clearing,
two naked feet the last Snub sees.

While she waits for Orphan to return
Snub looks out at shattered trees,
at plants mashed into the mud,
green merging with brown.

Orphan sees Snub's open eyes.
She exclaims and races over,
water leaking down her face
as she grooms Snub.

Snub tries to get up,
but the soreness in her throat
becomes a sharpness,
and the world goes white again.

The pain blooms white from her collarbone
whenever Snub moves,
so she holds perfectly still
and eats the sight of Orphan.

Snub does not feel *here.*
She is in her body and outside of it;
she is not Snub looking at Orphan,
but some bird looking at Snub
looking at Orphan.

Breath appears in front of Snub's eyes,
looking at her with fear and also longing.
Snub curls her lips in

acha

even though no sound can come out.

Breath sprawls along the ground,
pressing his back against Snub's thigh as hard as he can.
Even that small pressure causes the edge of her view
to go white,
but the comfort of Breath
is worth it.

Mother has her nose down
as she sifts through uprooted greens.
She hasn't gained any weight
since her time in the cavern.
Her shoulder blades rise from the
back of her rib cage
like fins.
Mother will never be fat again.

With her back against a tree trunk and
her head cradled in vines,
Snub can watch the magpies.
They are hopping about their nest.
Something inside it has them occupied.
This nest has eggs in it.
Eggs open into baby birds.
Maybe there will soon
be tiny magpies.

Those eggs are cozy and motionless.
Breath and Orphan are asleep.
Snub hears Mother eat
while she watches
the nesting magpies.

hoo.

Snub wakes to sunset drumming.

Maybe the not-gorillas are looking
for the corpse of their child.

Orphan startles and gets to her feet
while Breath clutches hard to Snub,
sending white lances down her side.

The sounds get louder.
The not-gorillas are coming.
Snub has always known they would.
The only option is to flee.

Snub cannot flee.
Mother cannot flee.

Orphan can flee.
Breath can flee.

Snub stares at Orphan and Breath.
Snub memorizes Orphan and Breath.

Orphan stands in the clearing,
gaze flicking between the drumming
and Snub,
understanding her kind and understanding Snub.

Breath presses his back tight against Snub,
as if to get all the way inside of her.

Mother eats.
Mother doesn't seem to mind the drumming.

Snub knows what she must do.
She raises the hand of her uninjured arm.
She pushes Breath away with all her might.

Breath squeals as he rolls in the dirt,
getting to all fours and glaring at Snub.

amrcha.

Snub bares her teeth at Breath,
makes a swiping gesture with her hand
toward the far side of the clearing.

Go.
I do not want you here.

Breath stares at her.
He is baffled.

Orphan is not like Breath.
Orphan can understand a future.
She steps toward Snub,
gibbering,
eyes wide and streaming water.

Breath takes a step toward Snub,
his body quivering.
Snub bares her teeth again
and waves him away.
If she could get to all fours
and chase him off,
she would.

Breath shrinks back from Snub.
Orphan, looking toward the calls
of the approaching not-gorillas,
reaches her arms out to Breath.

He ignores her at first.
Snub makes her sounds of

amrcha

even louder,
casts Breath away
even harder.

Breath allows his hand to be held by Orphan
while she tugs him to the far side of the clearing.
Breath's head tilts awkwardly so he can peer back

at Snub as he goes,
tripping over vines
for looking backward.

Orphan takes another step.
Breath again allows himself to be led.

Once they're at the far side of the clearing,
once they're about to pass out of view
forever
Breath yanks his hand out of Orphan's
and calls out

acha,

staring wildly at Snub.

Mother looks up, confused, then returns to her foraging.
Orphan takes Breath's hand back in hers,
tugs him out of the clearing,
away from the not-gorillas.

One more step, one more longing look back,
then Breath and Orphan have disappeared.

The last thing Snub sees of either of them
is two hands clasping,
gorilla and not-gorilla.

Breath is gone.
Snub makes an anguished cry,
and at the sound of it Mother
clicks and steps,
clicks and steps
until she's beside Snub.

Mother lowers herself to the ground,
joints creaking and protesting.

Mother grooms Snub.
Snub grooms Mother.

The earth and sky take turns
growing and shrinking
and ringing in Snub's ears.
She looks to the last place
she saw Breath and Orphan,
hoping for them to return.

But Snub knows that Orphan
will fight to live,
and that this means Orphan
and Breath
will not return.

The edges of the world remain white,
even when Snub keeps herself still.
She feels like she is floating again,

that she is like one of the magpies
watching Snub watch Mother.

She thinks of the nest,
looks up to see the birds
tending to their
home of sticks and spit,
which contains
the eggs
that contain
more magpies.

The magpies will stay with Snub and Mother.

Everything that exists in the world
has started to lull her.

Snub tucks Mother in closer,
treats Mother like she is Breath.

Mother does not seem to mind.
She gives out a long sigh
once she is fully in Snub's arms.

There are motes in the air,
bits of seed and pollen and feather
that catch the sunlight.

The air is thick with them,
a column of unsettled debris
that rises toward the sun.

The motes seem to throb
to the sound of the cicadas.
Over their drone,
Snub hears the
easy shallow breathing of Mother,
Snub's own pulse
sometimes quiet,
sometimes as loud as the drumming of the not-gorillas.

Snub's eyes have shut and will not open.

She does not want to open them.
In her mind is the image of Orphan and Breath,
leaving the clearing hand in hand.

That vision is all she sees,
and Mother is all she feels.

There are voices,
voices of strangers,
of not-gorillas,
both right here
and
far in the distance,
voices
that are everywhere
and
nowhere at all,
are now and before and to be.

One hand in another,
fingers gripping fingers,
Snub holds Mother,
Mother holds Snub.

Orphan and Breath are
young and agile,
small and strong.

By now
they will be far away,
finding a new home.

A Q&A WITH ELIOT SCHREFER

Q. It's not so often that a book's set in the paleolithic era. What inspired you to write this story in particular, rather than a book about modern gorillas?

A. I knew from the start that this book would feature gorillas, but everything else was up in the air. *Orphaned* is the last entry in a quartet of novels about the great apes. It all started with *Endangered* (a girl crosses wartime Congo while taking care of an infant bonobo), then *Threatened* (a boy survives the jungles of Gabon only by working his way into a group of chimpanzees), followed by *Rescued* (a boy is raised alongside an orangutan, until he breaks his ape brother out of confinement and goes on the run). As I was writing these books, I knew I would save the gorillas for last. There's something so noble and dignified about their calm demeanor—they're sort of like ape royalty to me.

I live in Manhattan, and the Bronx Zoo is just a subway ride away. I learned that if I got up early, arrived right at opening, and wore my running shoes, I could be by myself with the gorillas for about forty-five minutes before the rest of the zoo visitors got there. They're a rambunctious and charming family, and in those misty early-morning hours it felt like I was the out-of-place one, not the family of gorillas living in the big city.

At that same time, I was sitting on a book award jury, and my home was filled with teetering stacks of books. Amazing, beautiful books—but they all featured humans or animals that acted just like humans. I'd come home from those visits with these gorillas, with their specific and vivid personalities and their complicated emotions, and look at those books and think *novels are almost always about people!* I mean—obviously that's true, but it suddenly struck me as interesting.

This impulse to focus on the stories of our own species seems highly related to the ecological devastation we humans are wreaking on the planet. We are so dominant now that our actions can and do cause mass extinctions of species like the great apes. In the early years, though, our preeminence was far from a foregone conclusion. We were once pitiful compared to animals with strong teeth or fast legs or virulent poison or tough hides. What changed is that we learned to use tools, and use them well. Once we could use weapons to kill animals and eat meat, we got a surge of daily calories, which we could use to fuel our explosive brain growth. Brains are expensive organs—our 1450 cubic centimeter brain uses up 25 percent of our daily calorie intake.[1] (Gorillas, by comparison, have a much less costly 530 cc brain—despite having an average body mass that's twice ours.[2])

---

[1] *Nova: Becoming Human*, three-part documentary series.
[2] The University of Texas, Austin's efossils.org site: http://www.efossils.org/book /activity-3-relative-brain-size.

The early human story is thought to have involved a mass migration from Africa into Europe and the Middle East millions of years ago, followed by a return to Africa as tool-users around the time this book takes place. What culminated in our total dominance today started with a more neutral interaction hundreds of thousands of years ago. At some point, stronger gorillas must have had their first interaction with smarter humans. That first encounter really *happened*, somewhere, and once I realized that, I got fascinated by all the ways it might have played out.

Q. So Orphan and the "not-gorillas" were part of Snub's story from the very beginning?

A. Actually, no. Originally my idea was that a tool would accidentally come into the gorillas' possession, and that using this valuable object would become divisive and cause the gorillas to fracture, until a young gorilla goes on a journey to get rid of it and save her family. All well and good, except for a big problem: Once I started researching gorillas, I realized such a thing would never happen. Chimps, sure. Those clever and aggressive animals, so like us in all their competitive hysteria, would be perfect for a story like that. But a gorilla would look at a weapon, shrug, and go take a nap. They're far more interested in the important business of grooming and eating.

That's why the early humans became part of the novel. This ape quartet started with *Endangered*, about a human taking care of an orphan ape. I decided to take it full circle, and see how it might work the other way around, with a gorilla caring for a human. I wish we as a species could be nurtured by gorillas long enough to learn their greatest lesson: Take only what you need to survive, and leave the rest.

Q. And how about Snub in particular? How did you come up with her character?

A. Though young female gorillas leave their families to prevent inbreeding (just like in most every human culture throughout history), the gorilla herself would of course have no idea that was why she was leaving. Though natural selection is what gives Snub that drive, she'd have an emotional experience of it and not an intellectual one.

I started to wonder: What would be the gorilla's-eye view of leaving home? What would Snub be feeling that would cause her to forsake everything she's ever known and wander off?

She's basically Belle in the beginning of *Beauty and the Beast*, wanting "much more than this provincial life." Only she's a prehistoric gorilla with no singing voice. Otherwise just the same.

Q. How about Snub's name?

A. Gorillas all have distinctive nose-prints! It's how zookeepers and researchers tell them apart.

Q. Where should readers look to find out more about the "not-gorilla" early humans in the book?

A. There is still some debate about whether there's a meaningful distinction between the species *homo erectus* and *homo ergaster*. The two, previously thought to be genetically distinct populations, might actually be the same species of early human. In any case, they died out long enough ago (50,000 years ago at the latest) that it's hard to piece together much about their lives from the fossil record. Consensus is that they would have had a fine covering of hair over their bodies, with more on the top of their heads. Though it's unclear if the species had full language, they would almost certainly have communicated orally to some extent. They lived in collaborative groups, and might or might not have used fire—whether to cook (less likely) or to scare off predators (more likely). Anthropologists are pretty certain that they used simple tools in order to kill animals and also to skin them and wear their pelts, thereby avoiding the caloric cost of growing thick fur of their own—with the side benefit of allowing them to sweat more effectively, so they could run long distances to wear their prey down to exhaustion before the kill. Long-distance running is something we humans brought to the table.

The most famous *homo ergaster* is known as the "Turkana Boy," a fossil discovered in 1984 and the topic of Episode 2 of *Nova*'s excellent documentary series *Becoming Human*. Scientists have used the layers of enamel on his teeth to date him, and discovered he was a very large 5'3" upon his death at approximately age eight.

It's important to remember that humanness also added some moving, lovely qualities to the primate branch of life. We're not just jerks. The skeleton of an elder *homo ergaster* has been found that had been missing his teeth for two years before his death. Scientists postulate from that evidence that the others in his tribe might have chewed his food for him.[3] Gorillas haven't been observed doing similar; they will readily abandon other gorillas that get sick or infirm. Though humans have a higher capacity for interspecies violence than gorillas, they also have a higher capacity for caring, which I tried to capture in Orphan's surprising (to Snub) compassion for Mother. It's the paradox of humans: We really love animals even while we eat them and destroy their environment.

[3] *Nova: Becoming Human.*

Q. Scientists who write about the emotions of animals sometimes get accused of anthropomorphism, or erroneously assigning human qualities to animals that don't actually have them. Were you worried about that while trying to enter an animal's consciousness?

A. In researching gorillas, I leaned heavily on the writings of naturalist George Schaller, Dian Fossey's predecessor in studying gorillas in the wild. He was fascinated by the particularities of gorilla nature, and one of his lines always stuck with me: Unlike chimps, gorillas "are introverts, who keep their emotions suppressed. They retain their outward dignity when in fact they may inwardly be seething with excitement and turmoil."[4] Is this anthropomorphism? Or is it useful scientific observation?

There's a German word, *umwelt*, which, in the words of primatologist Frans de Waal, "stresses an organism's self-centered, subjective world, which represents only a small tranche of all available worlds."[5] In other words, to look into another animal's *umwelt* is to imagine how that animal sees the world. For example: A dog, with a nose more sensitive than its eyes, is getting more information about what's upwind of her than what's in front of her. Plenty of philosophers have tried to explore what another being's *umwelt* would be like, most famously Thomas Nagel in his 1974 essay "What Is It Like to Be a Bat?" Most thinkers writing about *umwelt* agree that any attempt must fail, that it's impossible to fully get over our own humanness. But I think it's no sin to try, and that attempting to imagine the point of view of "the other" is the best way we have to expand our empathy. As Joshua Rothman

[4]Schaller, *The Year of the Gorilla*, 228.
[5]Quoted in "The Metamorphosis: What Is It Like to Be an Animal?" by Joshua Rothman, *The New Yorker*, May 30, 2016.

put it, "In our efforts to imagine animal minds, there will always be a tension between sympathetic imagination and rational skepticism. Perhaps we should bend in the direction of sympathy."[6]

Q. Why poetry?

A. Back in May of 2016, thanks to a generous fellowship from the MacDowell Colony, I got to spend a month in a New Hampshire cabin, surrounded by forest. There I poured out Snub's story—in prose. When I gave the manuscript to my editor, David Levithan, he suggested that *Orphaned* might read better as poetry. I'd never have considered it, but when I thought about it, I realized he was right. There was something entirely too regimented—too human—about sentences and paragraphs. It worked against what I was trying to establish in inhabiting a gorilla consciousness. Poetry also allowed me more license to place the "gorilla vocalizations" I wanted to use along the right side of the page, and allowed me to use the gorilla images as openers for each poem.

Q. Tell us more about the pictures.

A. One thing that came out recurrently in my research was that gorillas are always attuned to their family group—their survival is closely tied to the group's survival, so they have an awareness of where the other gorillas in their group are at all times. Starting each poem with a "roll call" of sorts, identifying which gorillas were nearby, seemed a way to access that part of Snub's gorilla consciousness.

[6]Ibid.

Q. Some of the gorilla vocalizations have close equivalents in English. Why not just use more familiar words?

A. From all the literature of researchers who have studied gorillas in the wild, it seems pretty conclusive that they mourn, feel joy and envy, have playful and anxious sides. But that doesn't mean that a gorilla's sense of boredom (its "*hoo*") is just like a human's sense of boredom. Bertrand Russell once wrote that "boredom . . . consists in the contrast between present circumstances and some other more agreeable circumstances which force themselves upon the imagination."[7] Gorillas have no property and show little competition over items. If they live in the present, with no goals to acquire anything, then a simple and unchanging existence might not be stultifying at all—it might be the ultimate pleasure. Thus *hoo*, "acknowledging the peacefulness of a monotonous life." I'd like a lot more sense of *hoo* in my own existence, instead of that human ambition for more and more and more.

I guess the gorilla words were a way of reminding myself of everything that's unknowable about the gorilla.

As Schaller writes in *The Year of the Gorilla*, by spending his time with the gorillas in the jungle, he "found a freedom unattainable in more civilized surroundings, a life unhampered by a weight of possessions. We needed no keys to open locked doors or identification cards to obtain the things we desired. We, who had lived in America where the electric toothbrush and the battery-operated pepper grinder are becoming symbols of a civilization, moved backward in time to note with joy how little was needed for contentment. The beauty of the forest and the mountains laid claim to us, and as the days went

[7]Cited in Schaller, 177.

slowly by we came to live for the moment, taking limitless pleasure in the small adventures that came our way."[8] *Hoo*, indeed! And he didn't even have a smartphone to rail against.

Q. So, ever been through a volcanic eruption? For research?
A. Nope! And I'd prefer not to, thank you very much.

Q. Gorillas are highly endangered. How can people best help them today?
A. The quote that begins the novel is from an interview with Dian Fossey, who went into Rwanda in 1967 to study mountain gorillas and wrote one of the pioneering works of primatology, *Gorillas in the Mist* (later made into a film with Sigourney Weaver). Like Dr. Jane Goodall with the chimpanzees in Tanzania, Fossey's aim, through the support of anthropologist Louis Leakey, was to study the apes on their own terms and uncover what she could about how they lived in the wild. The resulting research was revolutionary in our knowledge about gorillas.

But as you can tell from Fossey's words, she began to have an easier time with the apes than with humans. She went to great lengths to protect the gorillas, in the process building a lot of animosity from the Rwandans around her. She was murdered on December 26, 1985, and the crime remains unsolved.

Fossey made the ultimate sacrifice for her cause, but luckily, there are many less costly ways to help! My sincere hope is that some young readers will devote their lives to conservation. That doesn't have to mean going into the field to do research and conservation, though

[8]Schaller, 154.

of course it can. The world's wildlife is also in desperate need of lawmakers, lawyers, and lobbyists—people who will work against the powerful economic interests that endanger them.

If you're not old enough for all that, there are still plenty of ways to help. Join one of the "Roots and Shoots" clubs the Jane Goodall Institute runs all over the world—and if there isn't one near you yet, contact them for information on how to start one! They undertake a mix of local and international projects, to help animals far away as well as in our own backyards. As a class or a school, you can also adopt an orphan gorilla through the Dian Fossey Gorilla Fund (gorillafund.org) or Gorilla Doctors (gorilladoctors.org) or Ape Action Africa (apeactionafrica.org) and help pay for the upkeep of an orphaned animal.

Q. Could you point readers where to look for more information?

A. Absolutely! Here are the resources that I found most useful in researching *Orphaned* (they are also the sources for the facts in this author's note). Those in **bold** are articles or documentaries especially suited to in-class use.

GORILLA PHYSIOLOGY AND BEHAVIOR

Among African Apes: Stories and Photos from the Field, edited by Martha M. Robbins and Christophe Boesch

The Education of Koko, by Francine Patterson and Eugene Linden

Gorilla, by Ian Redmond

Gorilla Behavior, by Terry L. Maple and Michael P. Hoff

Gorillas in the Mist, by Dian Fossey

Mountain Gorillas: Biology, Conservation, and Coexistence, by Gene Eckhart and Annette Lanjouw

Planet Ape, by Desmond Morris with Steve Parker

Virunga (documentary), directed by Orlando von Einsiedel

Walking with the Great Apes, by Sy Montgomery

The Year of the Gorilla, by George Schaller

UMWELT, OR IMAGINING GORILLA CONSCIOUSNESSES

"Are We in Anthropodenial?" by Frans de Waal, *Discover Magazine*, July 1997

"Can Fiction Show Us How Animals Think?" by Ivan Kreilkamp, *The New Yorker*, April 21, 2015

"Do Gorillas Even Belong in Zoos? Harambe's Death Spurs Debate," by Natalie Angier, *The New York Times*, June 6, 2016

"How do Gorillas Grieve?" an interview with Barbara King, *Pacific Standard*, June 9, 2016

"The Metamorphosis: What Is It Like to Be an Animal?" by Joshua Rothman, *The New Yorker*, May 30, 2016

"What Is It Like to Be a Bat?" by Thomas Nagel, *The Philosophical Review*, October 1974

VISITOR FOOTAGE FROM ZOOS
(hyperlinks available at www.eliotschrefer.com/gorillas)

"Gorilla playing 'peek-a-boo' with human toddler at the Columbus Zoo" (*Today* Show)

"Watch the enchanting gorillas who were VERY curious about a caterpillar" (DailyMail.co.uk)

"Wild gorillas compose happy songs that they hum during meals" (*New Scientist*)

HOMO ERGASTER AND EARLY HUMANS

Before the Dawn: Recovering the Lost History of Our Ancestors, by Nicholas Wade

Dragon Bone Hill: An Ice-Age Saga of Homo Erectus, by Noel T. Boaz and Russell L. Ciochon

Nova: Becoming Human, three-part PBS documentary series. Episode 2 deals most closely with *homo erectus* and *homo ergaster.*

VOLCANIC ERUPTIONS

Eruptions that Shook the World, by Clive Oppenheimer

The Great Rift: Africa's Greatest Story, BBC/Animal Planet documentary series. Episode I deals with how life adapted to the massive volcanic activity.

Super Volcano: The Ticking Time Bomb Beneath Yellowstone National Park, by Greg Breining

ACKNOWLEDGMENTS

The gorillas I visited at the Bronx Zoo should have been paid a consulting fee. But what's the point—if I gave them cash, they'd just eat it. Here are the not-gorillas I need to thank, though:

Sarah Mulhern Gross, an English teacher at High Technology High School in New Jersey, read a draft of this book and gave me many helpful thoughts on gorilla behavior—she observed them as part of her master's degree in conservation. She came up with the enticing idea that the fictional gorillas fleeing *homo ergaster* might have founded the small Congolese population of Grauer's gorillas, still alive today (though highly endangered).

Other early readers who helped me immensely with this book include Sy Montgomery, a longtime idol of mine who was generous enough to read a draft. I read her amazing *Walking with the Great Apes* as part of my research for *Endangered* six years ago, and for her to spend time reading my words now is a dream come true. Similarly, Dr. Jane Goodall's correspondence about *Rescued* led me in useful directions for this novel. Todd Mitchell, author of the fantastic *The Last Panther*, read an early draft of *Orphaned* and helped me to see how to shift the structure of the entire narrative to give it more shape. Donna Freitas, you helped me see this book in totally different ways over lunch. Daphne Benedis Grab, you helped me see it in a whole different set of ways over breakfast. Both were so helpful and so delicious. Patricia McCormick, I respect your work and your mind so much, and I'm so grateful for that lunch where we talked gorilla. (I'm realizing I eat a lot with my fellow authors.)

My longtime editor, David Levithan: You've seen these apes through from beginning to end, and I've come to rely on your strokes of genius. I feel very lucky to have someone with such good ideas in my corner.

Richard Pine, my agent: I'm a lucky, lucky primate to have an ally as terrific as you.

Thanks to the wonderful team at Scholastic, who work so hard to get books into the right hands. Lizette Serrano, Tracy van Straaten, Ellie Berger, Lori Benton, Emily Heddleson, Rachel Coun, Elizabeth Parisi, Maya Marlette, Melissa Schirmer, Alix Inchausti, Jazan Higgins, Sue Flynn, Nikki Mutch, Chris Satterlund, Barbara Holloway, Terribeth Smith, and many more: Thank you.

Thank you, MacDowell Colony, for the fellowship that allowed me to retreat into the woods to write. What a special place.

To my writer's group, Marianna Baer, Coe Booth, Anne Heltzel, Marie Rutkoski, and Jill Santopolo: You're such stalwarts. All times of year, through all sorts of restaurant closings and life upheavals and crazy New York weather, I can count on your kind faces and wise insights whenever I need them.

Family are my most constant readers: Mom, thanks for the check marks and smiley faces and your unfailing radar for word echoes. Eric Zahler, you're the emotional core of this book, and the source of much *acha*.

ABOUT THE AUTHOR

Eliot Schrefer's first three books in this quartet—*Endangered, Threatened,* and *Rescued*—count among them two finalists for the National Book Award, a New York Times Editors' Choice, two winners of the Green Earth Book Award, selection to the Amelia Bloomer List for best feminist works for young readers, and praise from Dr. Jane Goodall as being "moving, fascinating, and eye-opening." Schrefer is also the author of *The School for Dangerous Girls, The Deadly Sister,* two novels in the Spirit Animals series, and other books for children and adults. When he's not off somewhere hanging out with apes, he lives in New York City. Connect with him online at eliotschrefer.com.

READ ALL OF ELIOT SCHREFER'S
AWARD-WINNING APE QUARTET NOVELS